ĀASTIKA

THE BELIEVER

In Pursuit of Himalayan Spirituality

(MY WAY ON MY PLATE- PART-II)

Achyutt Daas

ĀSTIKA
The Believer
In Pursuit of Himalayan Spirituality
(MY WAY ON MY PLATE- PART-II)
Achyutt Daas

© Achyutt Daas

Published in 2024

© Published by

Qurate Books Pvt. Ltd.
Goa 403523, India
www.quratebooks.com
Tel: 1800-210-6527, Email: info@quratebooks.com

All rights reserved
No part of this publication may be reproduced, stored in a retrieval system, or transmitted in any form or by any means, electronic, mechanical, photocopying, recording or otherwise, without the prior permission of the author.

Disclaimer
This book is a fictional narrative based on the spiritual background of the Hindu philosophy, and all the characters in the book are fictional except for the revered ones in the sphere of Hindu religion and mythology. The fictional characters have no connection or resemblance to any person living or dead, to the best of the author's knowledge. Although every precaution has been taken to verify the accuracy of the information contained herein, the author/publisher takes no responsibility for any errors and omissions within.

ISBN: 978-93-58984-86-6

Dedication

Expressing my deepest gratitude to my parents late Shri Jatindra Chandra Das and late Smt Jayanti Das for my upbringing in a highly spiritual ambiance during my childhood, and further sending me to a highly disciplined ambiance of Army Boarding School, which made me what I am today – a highly independent person with an open mind, exploring truths of life.

I am deeply thankful to God – Lord Krishna, my childhood hero, and Lord Shiva from the second half of my life, for blessing me and getting me to where I am today on the righteous path to self-realization and consciousness.

The path is a long and arduous one, and the process of uncoupling the self from a limited mundane life to experiencing the unlimited consciousness of the universe is a tough one, but I am well on my way on the journey!

PROLOGUE

With a growing sense of disillusionment, Ved was thinking about the future course of his life. The spiritual journey of his life (as described in the Part-I of the book), was gradually stagnating, and he was getting nowhere further in life due to the distractions of mundane day to day routine chores.

Samsarik (worldly) activities shackled him like an octopus, contrary to providing him with clarity for the future course of his life.

He noticed that the volume of 'God Consciousness' in him was diminishing, and the present situation in his life overwhelmed him to such an extent that it became a constant nagging source of frustration.

He needed a fresh charge of God Consciousness, and he felt in his sub-conscious mind that a turning point in his life was imminent.

Something was about to happen, he felt.

And things did happen, that too sooner than he expected, something he least expected.

A massive earthquake measuring 6.5 on the Richter scale brought the entire hill-block on which Ved lived, down to shambles, and flattened to the ground level of the Bhimtal Lake, in the town of Bhimtal.

A series of events that followed after the earthquake later, became viral news that was narrated in the neighborhood over and over again - as God's miracle.

What had taken place that evening was that the horses in their stable had become restless and neighed frantically wanting to break free, and so did the cows in their shed. The dogs barked incessantly; it took Ved and Malti only a few moments to realize that some sort of a natural disaster was imminent.

Ved hurriedly came to calm down the animals as best as he could, and then guided them to the meditation-dome at the far eastern corner of the hill. He did the same with the dogs, and also the people who lived there.

Ved, and Malti were surprised to note that all the animals became calm and behaved normally once they were inside the meditation-dome as if they felt protected there.

And just as Ved managed to gather everyone inside the dome, all hell broke loose. The hill collapsed as if sucked in by a gigantic vacuum machine; flattening the entire hill to the level of the ground.

What was even more astonishing was that the meditation-dome where Ved and others including all the animals took shelter remained untouched!

The meditation-dome stood alone like a space needle on a sixty feet tall circular tower. The local people compared the scene with that of Hanuman holding aloft an entire hillock on his fingers like in the Hindu epic Ramayana.

The meditation-dome stood atop a sixty feet tall pillar, and looked like a floating lounge. It was a sight to behold.

A miracle had just happened, and this news spread like wildfire. The press and media reporters converged at this quaint little sleepy town of Bhimtal to witness the God-show that happened there.

The spectacle of Ved, Malti, and others inside the meditation-dome looked as if they were floating in the sky. It was like a scene from a science fiction movie.

It was not about assessing the damages caused by the earthquake that was being talked about by the people, it was about how a place of spiritual practice remained unharmed when everything around it had collapsed to the ground.

This incident received widespread media attention, and a discussion ensued in the religious circles, whether it was really an act of God or not. This was definitely an incredible sight captured live that aroused a lot of sensation.

Ved and Malti became instant celebrities and were declared as 'Angels of God'.

When the news reached Yukta, Yamini, and many others who were Ved's disciples, they flew into Bhimtal to take stock of the situation and ensure that Ved and Malti were safe.

Ever since the incident had taken place, the media covered the story 24x7 with a magnifying glass trying to analyze what had taken place inside the meditation hall before, during and after the earthquake. Each and every move made by Ved and Malti were being duly reported.

The survivors had to remain atop, inside the meditation-dome, for the next three days. Meanwhile, experts were deployed to assess the safety around the land where the dome stood; to confirm if it was strong enough to be approached for the rescue operation.

On the third day the green signal was given to the rescue team to go ahead with the rescue operation, to evacuate everyone from the meditation-dome.

It took about 8 hours of serious hard work on the part of the disaster management team to rescue Ved, and all the others including the animals.

The evacuation process for the animals proved to be a tough job. But the job was eventually accomplished successfully.

The rescued people were immediately shifted to a hospital for medical care and checkup, and then to a government guest house after that.

To the astonishment of all those present at the site, yet another miracle manifested – soon after everyone was rescued, the dome and the pillar crumbled! The dumbfounded onlookers couldn't believe their eyes and gazed in shock.

The local folks took care of the horses, cows, dogs and all other animals and were treated as if they too were a part of divinity.

Thousands of people from places all around visited Bhimtal daily and conducted prayers, kirtan, and havan ceremony (mass religious fire rituals) as an acknowledgement of what they interpreted as the divine act of God manifestation at Bhimtal.

Ved had to struggle to restrain these people from going overboard on superstitious beliefs, and tried hard to convince them that they were ordinary people just like the others.

Ved's cousin once again came to help them, and he persuaded them to shift to his home till some other arrangements were made.

Life for Ved and Malti became quite difficult in the aftermath of the incident due to incessant interference by numerous social organizations and the media, and hence they decided to slip out of Bhimtal quietly, unannounced. He took his cousin into confidence and worked out a plan. His cousin agreed to let them go and assured them that he would look after the horses, cows, and the dogs while they were away.

Ved asked Yukta, Yamini, and their friends to go back, assuring them that they would remain in touch. But they decided to stay back for some more time in Bhimtal.

As planned, Ved and Malti moved out early in the morning on the next day, around 4 am, under the cover of darkness.

His cousin drove them to kathgodam - the nearest rail station to Bhimtal, and from there Ved and Malti took a bus to travel towards Gobindghat – up on the hills in the state of Uttarakhand - also known as the 'Abode of the Angels'.

And amidst the rapidly changing course of events, all that occupied Ved's and Malti's mind was the 'Mountain Man'.

Ved desperately wanted to meet the Mountain Man to get some answers regarding whatever that was happening in their lives, and for what purpose.

His recollection of the last encounter with the Mountain Man was still fresh in his mind. He remembered what the Mountain Man had said about one's predestined sequence of events that were bound to happen during the course of one's life, and those events which defined their destiny.

The Mountain Man had clarified that the pre-scripted destiny was in fact born out of the person's own accumulated karma from past lives, and the person's present life is an ongoing process of evolution of newer karma in the present life, for achieving a higher self.

While most people curse their fate for the difficult situations in life, spiritual philosophy looks at it in a complete opposite manner. Spiritualism in fact invites such difficult situations in life as a stepping-stone to conquer higher levels of empowerment, and to evolve to become a superior self.

A famous Urdu Sufi poet beautifully coined the following words – *'Dard se mera daaman bhar do, O' Allah!'* sung by the legendary Indian singer late Lata Mangeshkar. It was a prayer to God asking Him to fill her life with all the pains and sorrows of the world, and in exchange make the world a happier place to live.

The basic philosophy being that, the fruits of hard work and pain bear the fruit of joy and happiness. Sacrifices made for the good of others, and abstinence from self-gratification can compel God to give in to the devotee's wishes.

It is only when one lives in a state of abstinence, or in a state of deprivation, that one can truly pursue a spiritual journey. When desires are crushed, the ego is not allowed to raise its ugly head, then one learns to accept God's providence with complete surrender. Then one's prayers are answered. Thus, one learns to live a life of austerity, and remain focused on the primary goal – that of seeking the truth.

Ved had never hungered for wealth, or fame. He knew that he was part of a superior game plan, and a superior power was guiding the course of his life. Yet he felt insecure and uncertain, not knowing what lay ahead of him in the future.

This was the second time around, that life had presented him with a challenging situation and a formidable one at that; one which would take him to attain yet another higher level of consciousness.

The first time when Ved had been traumatized was when he had lost his entire family in an accident. That had led to his meeting with the 'Mountain Man'. The Mountain Man had guided him with a new purpose and identity. He had also got his life partner Malti amidst the course of changing times. The Mountain Man as his guru and mentor was a priceless gift from God.

This time around, with all his property snatched away by the earthquake, he had become homeless. The only saving grace was that they had come out unscathed. This by itself was a miracle of God, one that Ved and Malti acknowledged with deep gratitude.

Hence Ved realized that this new turn of events would pave way to the next phase along the journey of his soul i.e to graduate to a higher plane of consciousness!

Hence, he silently acknowledged, accepted the turn of events, and thanked God for the same with deep gratitude.

***

Contents

CHAPTER I: Ved's Moment Of Truth 15

CHAPTER II: Walking The Path To Freedom - Discovering The Subtle Self 27

CHAPTER III: Twin Flame – 'Ardha-Narishwar' Indoctrination Of Ved & Malti At Triyugi Narayan And Gupt Kashi 37

CHAPTER IV: Vedic Covenant Of Marriage 55

CHAPTER V: Dev Bhoomi – The Himalayas 63

CHAPTER VI: Initiation Into The Plane Of Angels At Kailash Parvat 85

CHAPTER VII: Kumbh Mela (The Kumbh Fair) 93

CHAPTER VIII: The Conspiracy 109

CHAPTER IX: Aastika - The Believers 131

CHAPTER X: In The Footprints Of The Himalayan Masters - 139

CHAPTER XI: Panorama Of Hindu Faith –
An Amazing Canvas Of
Temples, Gods And Godesses 151

CHAPTER -XII: The School Of Elders 169

EPILOGUE 173

Chapter I
VED'S MOMENT OF TRUTH

Conversations with the Mountain Man

As planned, Ved's cousin took them to Kathgodam, (the nearest railhead at the foothills of Nainital) and later dropped them at the Kathgudam bus station.

Ved and Malti boarded a bus the next day for Govind Ghat on their way to the 'Valley of Flowers', hoping that somehow, they would be able to meet the Mountain Man there.

The Valley of Flowers was a difficult place to reach. One had to drive up to the nearest point called Govind Ghat and then a trek for about 16 Kms on foot to reach there.

After a seven-hour bus ride, they reached Govind Ghat the same evening. They took a room at a guest house and rested for the night.

Ved felt a lot better after reaching Govind Ghat. His fears and anxiety gradually started dissipating in anticipation of meeting the Mountain Man through whom he could get to know about their future life.

The Valley of Flowers is aptly called as heaven on Earth due to its sublime beauty, ambience, and spectacular breathtaking aura. Its unique feel of divinity has earned for itself the recognition of a world heritage status. It is located at a height of about 3,660 meters above the sea level and is a vast spread of about 90 sq.mtr of wilderness with hundreds of species of floral bounty and fauna, with a breath-taking natural landscaping, which is nothing short of being one of the amazing sights of the world. The non-motorable approach and the16 Kms trek to reach the valley has ensured the sanctity of the place and protected the place from human interference, and hence retained its natural virgin-glory through the centuries. The trek to the valley goes through dense forests, along the river Pushpavati and can be reached by crossing several bridges and waterfalls along the way.

After having a night's rest, Ved and Malti set out on foot for the 16 Km trek to the Valley of Flowers, early in the morning next day. They had their backpacks, carrying all the essentials and including some food and water.

Four-five hours later, they arrived at their destination.

Here time stood still, as they simply got lost in the amazing ambiance of silent bliss and beauty! The hissing sound of air was music to their ears. All their tiredness after their hilly trek vanished and they felt completely lost in a state of ecstasy. An awesome feeling of limitlessness overpowered their senses, and their minds became thoughtless, as if they were consumed into an infinite space of endless universe. Having lost all of their senses amidst the beauty, fragrance, and grandeur of the Eden on Earth, they relished every breath they took, and waited expectantly for some more wonders to unfold. They now had nothing to worry about, as they felt they were a tiny spec in the midst of awe and beauty.

It was late in the afternoon. They were sitting on a wooden log and resting, when out of nowhere a booming voice of someone shook them out of their reverie. And just as Ved had anticipated, a surprise was waiting for them at the Valley of Flowers. He recognized the voice of the Mountain Man as he heard his name being called out by someone from a distance in the woods.

As they looked around, all of a sudden, the tall figure of the Mountain Man stood right in front of them!

"Hello my friend," the mountain man greeted. "I thought you wanted to meet me, didn't you Ved?" Ved was taken aback at the realization that the Mountain Man knew all along, about the inner turmoil he was going through, and that he was seeking help from him.

"Yes, indeed!" Ved replied shyly. "I was hoping you would show up here."

"It's a real pleasure to meet you Malti," the Mountain Man continued. "Ved must have spoken to you about me, didn't he?"

"Yes, yes of course!" Malti fumbled for words.

"Indeed," the Mountain Man replied. "It was about time I met you. But you two seem to be at some crossroads at the moment; is that why you wanted to see me?"

"Ah, I guess that's true," Ved replied.

Malti was completely nonplussed at the turn of events and looked dumbfounded in the presence of the Mountain

Man – a giant of a man and yet so soft in nature, his glowing radiant face with an overwhelming aura that appeared to pervade everything around him, including themselves.

The Mountain Man was aware of the impact he was having on Malti.

"Tell me, how has been the journey of your life with Ved," he asked. "You two were attracted to each other like magnets when you met at the charity fair?"

Malti's mouth opened in a gasp at the realization that he knew everything about them.

"Since you know everything about us, did you also play a role in uniting Ved and me?" asked Malti.

"Not really, I am just an emissary," the Mountain Man replied. "Well, you were destined to reunite, since you two are about to complete your nuptial vows for the seventh time in succession!

"Soon we all are about to become compatriots, after the rituals of your Twin-Flame (Ardha-Narishwar) indoctrination rituals are performed at the holy site of Gupt Kashi and Triyugi Narayan."

Malti and Ved were too shocked to react to what the Mountain Man had just said, and they looked on blankly.

Seeing the blank expression on their faces, the Mountain Man explained – "When a man and a woman complete seven consecutive married lifetimes together, they attain parity in terms of the male and female Tatva (of Shiva and Shakti). In simple terms, the two soul mates harmonize to become one soul – called a God Child."

In Hindu philosophy, Samsara is a balance of two forms of energy – Purush and Prakriti. Purush is male energy (Pingla) and Prakriti (nature) is female energy (Ida) – just as Yin and Yang in Chinese philosophy. Ida is feminine energy as is the Moon, and Pingla is masculine, as is the Sun. Each one is incomplete without the other, and hence need to be in harmony for sustenance of our eco system. The system of marriage is one of God's gift to humanity for the sustenance of the human-eco system.

Marriage is an integral part of 'The School of Life' where both the partners get to evolve to a higher self by adapting to the wisdom of the other form of energy and becoming a wholesome balanced self.

This is also known as the state of 'Ardha-Narishwar' when the two individuals (souls) become soulmates and a Twin Flame.

> The soulmates after spending seven lifetimes devoting completely to the ideology of self-growth by living together as a husband and wife, can evolve to become a perfect soul – a God Child!
>
> Ref to the Indian tradition of taking the marital vows by walking seven times around the Holy fire of the Yajna (Havan Kund) to take the vows, amidst the chanting of 'Slokas' (mantra) by the priest.

The seven consecutive conjugal lifetimes spent together, is like a progressive ovulation process when the two souls absorb the essence of each other, which leads to the creation of a common balanced mindset – neither male, nor female. This uniformity of a balanced 'male-female' mindset manifest into a superior soul, and new independent God-Child is born.

The newborn soul- the God-Child, is capable of dwelling with or without a human body, and can choose to pursue a field of Karma either in the physical world, or in the "Shukshma" microcosmic world – based upon the continuity of the preceding Karma of the couple.

"I hope I have cleared most of your confusion Ved," the Mountain Man asked.

"I am grateful to you for clearing my confusion," Ved replied. "I seem to have lost my bearings somewhat, and hence was a quite restless. The earthquake was unnerving!"

"Don't worry Ved," the Mountain Man replied. "It's quite natural for you to become restless at times like this, but rest assured, the next phase of your journey has just begun, and you will have more challenging tasks ahead of you at the next 'Kumbh Mela' to be held at Rudra Prayag.""Mahavatar Babaji has chosen you, and has specially asked me to come to meet you, to share his blessings," revealed the Mountain Man.

Ved was completely taken by surprise after hearing this, and wondered as to how the ensuing new phase of their life would be like.

Hundreds of questions sprung up in his mind – would they become one person after the Ardha-Narishwar ceremony at Triyugi Narayan, or would they remain as two different individuals as before? What are the expected changes that are likely to happen?

Similar mental imagery flooded Malti's mind too. Both of them were lost in the torrent of their own thoughts.

The Mountain Man was amused seeing them in such a state.

"You two need to cheer up! You have to tune up your perception levels for the next higher phase of life. The blessings of Mahavatar Babaji will guide you on," he said. "I too am available around you whenever the need arises. I am your partner in this."

The Mountain Man continued, "Babaji feels that the time is perfect for you two to experience the 'Bairagya' stage prior to your indoctrination ceremony."

Bairagya is a stage when one frees the self from the four walls of one's home, and all forms of association of familial life, and is considered as a pre-trial experience for a person for achieving Moksha (eternal freedom), and hence achieve Nirvana.

Bairagya also is a state of 'Pratyahara' - the fifth state of the Ashtanga Yoga, when one learns to un-couple/disconnect from worldly attachments - to enable the self to focus on the higher realms of consciousness.

Though Malti was not too comfortable at hearing this, Ved appeared to be quite comfortable with the thought, as if he was anticipating such a transition for quite some time, and everything now fell into place.

Ved was pleased at the thought that they were now graduating to the next higher level, and was anxious to know as to what lay ahead.

The Mountain Man was pleased to see the thoughts playing in Ved's mind, and said – "This is a well-deserved transition Ved, only a few achieve this landmark in a century.

"This will be a transition like nothing you have experienced before. This is a transcendence to a higher plane of 'Nirgun' and 'Niraakar' – a plane of dwelling without any shape and size; which literally means when one does not conform to any expression of description - one who becomes a part of the limitlessness- like the infiniteness of the universe.

"You no longer will have any references to the 'mind-ego' concept anymore. You will merge and become one with the creator. You will forfeit all human traits such as hunger and thirst, and will no longer be under the spell of time and space. You will experience a completely new 5th dimension of the universe, where each and every speck of your consciousness will be multi-dimensional!"

Ved and Malti listened in apt silence, as the Mountain Man continued - "No one can attain Nirvana by remaining attached to Samsarik (human eco system) ties, or bondage to any relationship. And you can't shelve your ego by remaining as a part of the Samsara – the world of Maya.

"Bairagya, and Vanaprastha are a way to gain freedom from the world of Maya and illusion that shackles you to think that your name or the body is the real you.

"When you lose your identity, the 'I' is shelved. Then you practically experience detachment by becoming nameless and are able to throw yourself in to the lap of the limitless universe. Only then can you experience the essence of real freedom i.e Nirvana.

"And most importantly, it introduces you to the universality of the soul – which is your true identity."

"The earthquake made it happen for you," the Mountain Man continued. "How else would you have experienced this unless you freed yourself from the home that imprisoned you, and stopped you from getting your freedom?

"The earthquake released you from all your bondage, and now you are on your way to experiencing what real freedom felt like.

"Yes, this journey is not so simple, let me warn you both, because tough situations will test your faith every now and then. But your faith and trust will see you through all such situations.

"And you will learn that the fear is not an issue, because it's only the body that fears, not your true self."

The Mountain man took a pause and looked at Ved and Malti.

"Do you get the picture now?" asked the Mountain Man.

Both Ved and Malti nodded silently, not knowing about the enormity of what lay ahead. But they understood everything it implied.

"Rest assured," the Mountain Man added further. "You have nothing to worry about, as God always take care of His children, and you have Mahavatar Babaji's blessings too. You already have had the first-hand experience of how you were protected during the earthquake, didn't you?"

They didn't need any more assurance now and wanted to fall at his feet to take his blessings for their next venture as selfless wanderers in the vast wilderness – two free souls with not a care in the world.

Lost in their thoughts, they didn't even notice that the Mountain Man was gone.

Now it became clear to Ved as he realized the reason why he was guided by the Mountain Man to come to the Valley of Flowers – to unfold for them their future, and counsel them about the next phase of their life's journey.

He wanted to enlighten them about the concept of Bairagya for shelving the "I" from the self, to experience the essence of eternal freedom - Nirvana.

A smile appeared on Ved's face as the realization hit home - that they were tiny players in the theatre of life playing just a role – that they were just puppets dancing to the strings pulled by the Master - the words of Shakespeare!

Malti was surprised seeing the smile on Ved's face - here they were at a crucial re-defining moment in their life, and he was smiling!

***

Chapter II

Walking the Path to Freedom - Discovering the Subtle Self

And thus began their journey of life on an uncharted course, picking up the pebbles of wisdom along the way.

Ved and Malti were already well on their way to make a start to the next phase of their life – a journey that would take them from a gross level of existence to a subtler level of existence, to experience the essence of freedom in the real sense of the term.

The abrupt disappearance of the Mountain Man at the Valley of Flowers left Ved and Malti in a state of void, as if they lost the last straw they were clinging onto. And then the realization sunk in, that it was their game now and they were all on their own from now on.

Ved and Malti spent a few days more at the famous Sikh Shrine "Hemkunt Sahib" at Govind Ghat. They were given a room to stay, and as was the system at all Sikh shrines, 'Langar-Prasad' (food) was freely available for everyone.

The peace and tranquility at the shrine was anointing and gave them a sense of Godspeed for their future.

Both Ved and Malti now allowed the thought of living the life of a monk, sink in into their minds, and to do that what could be a better place than at this pristine shrine of Guru Hemkunt Sahib?

Now, on retrospection about everything that the Mountain Man had said, Ved realized that they were asked to empower their spiritual energies to an optimum level by rigorous meditation and breath control techniques to be able to sustain themselves amidst the numerous odds that they might face each passing day while wandering around and learning to become a part of the wilderness in a broader perspective.

A couple of months passed by and both Ved and Malti began to feel the fervor of vibrancy from within, once again. A unique sense of freedom lifted their spirits, encouraging them to walk into the welcoming arms of the unknown. They began to feel the lightness of the freedom and unaccountability, and a kind of exultation arose from the feeling of assurance that they were now constantly being looked after, by loving Mother Nature.

They mostly travelled from one shrine to another - sometimes on foot and on other occasions by bus or train.

Thanks to the advances of the modern times, Ved could withdraw money from the ATM machine whenever he needed.

Having spent the first few months of their initial life as wandering monks visiting the 'Char-Dham' – the four pilgrimage sites of Hindu culture (Kedarnath, Badrinath, Gangotri, and Yamunotri), they then proceeded to the famous Jageswar Dham, a shrine located about 20 Kms away from the hilly township of Almora.

Jageswar Dham is also considered as the fifth prominent pilgrimage after the four Dhams (shrines) mentioned above.

Jageswar Dham is a cluster of about 125 temples in one compound, the main one being that of Adi Yogeswar Mrityunjai Shiva – the parent representation of the 12 main Jyotirlingas spread all across India.

The shrine is surrounded by thick jungles of Deodar trees (Cedar), and a hilly Jharna (Spring water) flowing by next to it. Lord Shiva is said to have meditated at this site around in the 7th century BCE.

The place is charged with divine energies and vibrations. Just by being there one is filled with positivity, and pious thoughts. The beauty and silence of the place is so subtle that it connects to one's soul consciousness instantly and filled it with divinity!

Ved and Malti too felt the bliss instantly, and a feeling of some inspiration filled their heart.

Malti saw the gleam in Ved's eyes and asked him about it.

Ved explained to her that this was the place where they would be able to learn a lot of ancient wisdom from the direct descent 'Avatar' of Lord Shiva, i.e Mahavatar Babaji.

Ved and Malti settled down fully convinced that they would be here for a long haul.

They found themselves a decent room at the nearby 'Dharamshala' (lodge meant for wandering monks).

Food was plentifully available. The place was heavenly, except for the lack of cleanliness in the lodge, particularly the bathrooms. But that did not deter their spirit, as they decided to tackle the issue themselves by cleaning and washing the bathrooms and the dining room. When others saw them doing the cleaning, they too followed the trend, and the place became like home.

They soon became popular with the nearby villagers as Ved and Malti took keen interest in educating the village children. Some elderly men and women too often sought their counsel and sat with them for discussing spiritual topics.

Their day started at 4 am in the morning with a prolonged spell of 'Dhyana' (meditation) for two hours, then they attended the 'Aarti' (prayer ceremony) conducted by the temple priest at 6.30 am which lasted for about an hour. They then spent a few hours educating the villagers and their children till the noon usually sitting under the shades of a huge neem tree with a span of about 40 feet shade coverage.

They rested for an hour or so in the afternoon after enjoying some 'Bhog Prasad' offered at the temple that were donated by the devotees to the temple.

Their evenings were spent in 'Puja' (ritual) ceremonies at the temple, or in 'Japa' (chanting of mantras) sessions.

Once a week, they assembled for 'Sat-sang' (spiritual communion) in the village *Chaupal* (community center).

And as time passed by, Ved and Malti gradually became attached to their settled routines that they were following at the Jageswar Dham.

And just when Ved was becoming aware of this fact, one fine day an unexpected event took place.

Ved was sitting on the temple compound looking at the setting Sun, when he experienced a strange transformation – as if an entire book of information became visible to him in a flash. He felt dizzy, and then he fainted.

Some people noticed him and revived him by sprinkling water on him. On coming awake, he felt as if a heavy load of software had got download into his memory; Mahavatar Babaji's art of 'Kriya Hatha Yoga' was revealed to him by an act of divinity!

In the meantime, someone informed Malti that something had happened to Ved. She rushed immediately to find Ved sitting on the floor looking at the sky in a state of daze.

It took him a while to absorb the enormity of what he had just learnt, and when he saw Malti, he clung on to her for a few minutes and then whispered into her ear as to what had happened. And he went on to blurt out in one go, the entire concept and techniques of Mahavatar Baba Ji's Kriya Hatha Yoga that Mahavatar Babaji had infused into him.

He explained to Malti that the concept of unification of the Sun and the Moon was the basic fundamental principle of 'Hatha Yoga' – the union (Yoga) of the 'spirit' and the 'nature', or unification of the Yang and the Yin (the energies of the male and the energies of the female shakti), without which a tug of war prevailed, and perfection could never be achieved.

'Hatha Yoga' – 'Ha' means the Sun or the Ying, and 'Tha' means the Moon- the Yin; and Yoga is the unification of the two.

Hatha Yoga takes off from where Patanjali's Yoga Sutras (Ashtanga Yoga) end; and is more of a Tantrik procedure as it unifies the mental aspects with the Prana (life force energies)- the two forms that of the male energies and the female energies that flow through the subtle Ida channel and the Pingala channel in the spinal cord.

The harmony of these two energies activates the 'Kundalini' energies to be awakened to manifest the 'self-realization' of the person. The awakening of Kundalini requires a higher level of physical as well as mental fitness to absorb the intense level of energies that arises in the body.

Kriya Hatha Yoga (KHY) is a tough procedure involving physical kriyas, meditations, pranayamas that could take the practitioner to a yet another level of expanded consciousness.

The Hatha Yoga practitioner has to master the physical body and the mental body to be able to sustain the self in a prolonged state of transcendence from the physical consciousness of the self.

Kriya Hatha Yoga can take us to the ultimate level of experience - not just of the mind, but to an extraordinary 'body-mind' psychokinetic experience involving every cell and tissue in the body to attain freedom from the ego, and to an awakened state of selflessness, self-realization or enlightenment.

When an ego-free practitioner goes through the rigorous techniques of Kriya Hatha Yoga, he can bring about achieving unusual powers that no ordinary person can ever achieve.

The main Kriyas (practices) of KHY are -

- Asana (postures)
- Sat-Karma (cleansing of thoughts and actions)
- Pranayama (controlled breathing exercises)
- Mudra (energy seal)
- bandh (energy locks), and
- Samadhi – the subsequent state of self-realization and enlightenment.

'Asana' - yogic posture, is a procedure that stimulates various parts of the body and creates relaxation after removing the stiffness and the blocks in the central nervous system.

'Sat-Karma' and Pranayamas, also known as the 'Sat-kriyas' are kriyas that are meant for purification of the body to prepare for the actual Yoga (Union).

The 'Svatmantrama', as they are outlined as, are Neti, Dhauti, Nauli, Basti, Kapal Bhati, and Trataka.

'Mudra' is a procedure which allows abundant flow of Prana, and since the five forms of Prana constitute the living form, there are numerous Mudras (unique postures of the fingers) for activating the different types of Pranas at different parts of the body. This, in simple terms is a procedure which removes blockages of energy flow across the body via the network of the 72,000 nada channels and the psyche.

Bandh is a psycho-muscular energy-lock procedure which helps in regulation of the prana energies by the self, to stimulate the Seven Chakras (the psycho energy distribution centers) to enhance the transmission of the Pranic energies in the body.

This advanced form of yoga has been passed on through the centuries, and in the 20th century by Paramhans Yogananda ('Autobiography of a Yogi' book), and till recently as illustrated by Michel Govindan (author of the book 'Babaji') a lineage disciple of Swami Yogananda Paramhansa.

The significant aspect of Kriya Hatha Yoga, as propounded by the ancient 'Siddhas' (sages) lay in the Yoga- the association of the yogic Asanas with an adjunct to Pranayama with various techniques of inhalation and exhalation, which results in a state of meditative consciousness.

Kriya Hatha Yoga helps in integrating the assertive, masculine and rational wisdom with the receptive and intuitional 'Shakti' aspect of feminine – the Yin, and the Yang.

A lack of balance between the masculine and feminine energies of the self, causes a depletion of Prana's flow in the body.

Kriya Hatha Yoga eliminates this imbalance and releases the energy blocks in the channels, also known as the 'Nadas'.

As the primary objective of all yogic practices are for development, maintenance, and welfare of the body, mind, and the soul for a healthy and prosperous human eco-system (Samsara); the prevention and cure of diseases and ailments are a must.

The postures (Asanas), the Bandhs, and the Mudras bring about a harmony and relaxation on all five planes by massaging the internal organs and glands to stabilize the physical body.

They prevent and cure many physical disorders, as well as mental disorders.

Thus, Yoga eliminates ailments of both – physical and mental.

Nurturing the 'Jeeva' (the seed of life) and developing an awareness of our life force energies (Prana) can take us a long way in the journey of life, no matter the ways and means we take, as long as they are learnt from a master.

Here the practitioners of yoga need to be cautioned about the wrongs that can happen if practiced in a wrong manner, because the correct control and management of one's inner energies are of vital importance. The flow of energies must be in the right direction.

Though yoga is a non-invasive technique, the psychic and emotional aspects of yoga need to be understood properly so as to apply them adequately.

A wrongfully aroused Kundlini energy can make a person go insane, and that happens quite often.

After having blurted out all of it, Ved paused and tried to compose himself.

Malti felt numb and looked on in disbelief. She soon understood why Ved was imparted with the knowledge of Kriya Hatha Yoga by Mahavatar Babaji. She also understood that the wisdom had to be imparted to her by Ved, so that every cell in her body absorbed the wisdom completely.

And both accepted with grace and gratitude Babaji's directives to propagate Kriya Hatha Yoga for the wellbeing of the people.

They began their first initiation of Babaji's Kriya Hatha Yoga there itself. They randomly welcomed about 15 villagers - both men and women and proceeded to teach them in detail how to incorporate Kriya Hatha Yoga into their lives in a holistic manner.

It was a big success, and they felt the presence of Mahavatar Babaji during the entire process of initiation.

Then Ved decided to impart the initiation to Yukta and Yamini also, and to the other members of their group whom Ved had taught the nine-day mental and physical fasting techniques.

For this, Ved invited them to come to a place called Gupt-Kashi near Kedarnath- one of the Char-Dhams of the four Hindu shrines.

Little did he know at that time that this would turn out to be an invitation to Yukta, Yamini, and their other friends, for their own Twin-Flame indoctrination ceremony!

***

Chapter III

TWIN FLAME – 'ARDHA-NARISHWAR' INDOCTRINATION OF VED & MALTI AT TRIYUGI NARAYAN AND GUPT KASHI

Gupt Kashi is a small hilly town located at an elevation of about 1,319 meters in the Kedarnath region in the Garhwal district in the Himalayas, in India. The historical reference of Gupt Kashi relates to the Vishwanath temple, an avatar of Lord Shiva of the famous temple at Kashi Vishwanath, Varanasi, in the state of Uttar Pradesh.

Gupt Kashi has quite a few anecdotes attached to it associated with Lord Shiva. As the name suggests – 'Gupt' means a hidden secret, and Kashi refers to Kashi Vishwanath of Varanasi – a highly revered pilgrimage center of Lord Shiva.

The first reference was about how Lord Shiva hid inside a cave at Gupt Kashi when he wanted to make himself unavailable to the Pandavas (of the Hindu epic

Mahabharata), who wanted his blessings to enable them to enter the heaven to attain Moksha. The story goes that later Lord Shiva appeared, but not in one form, but in five parts – each one part of his body appeared at five different places – known as 'Panch-Kashi'.

The second anecdote, and a more relevant one, was that Parvati proposed to Lord Shiva after she elevated her consciousness level to a 'Daivik' (Angelic) level after thousands of years of 'Tapasya' (meditative state to acquire Daivik consciousness) at Gauri Kund – a small lake 17 Kms from Kedarnath, the famous pilgrimage site. When Lord Shiva agreed to accept Parvati as his wife, the marriage was performed by Lord Brahma acting as the priest, and Lord Vishnu acting as Mata Parvati's brother. All the Devtas (angels), and Rishis participated in this marriage ceremony, and which has since been the bible for the ritualistic covenants of a Hindu marriage. The fire at the altar of the Havan Kund that was lit for the marriage has been burning through the past three Yugs, and is still seen alight at Triyugi Narayan temple, where the marriage took place. The marriage platform is still revered by the people and is known as 'Brahmsheela'. There are three smaller Kunds (ponds) where Brahma, Vishnu, and the Devtas bathed prior to the marriage ceremony. These are known as Brahma Kund, Vishnu Kund, and Rudra Kund. The water to all the three Kunds come from the river Saraswati. They still exist even today.

It is said that if a childless couple bathes in any one of these Kunds and seek blessings for a child, their wish is always fulfilled.

And it's a common belief that any couple who visit the site of the marriage at Triyugi Narayan and take Babhoot (ash) from the 'Akhand-Agni' (the fire that has been alight since the last three yugas), they are blessed with a divine matrimonial bliss and harmony.

And needless to say, that this place has ever since been a sought-after wedding destination for those who are familiar with the famous union of Shiva and Parvati.

This was the first time ever that a union between a subtle non-physical entity (Shiva), and a person of gross physical form - Goddess Parvati, was performed by God Brahma, and God Vishnu acting as the bride's brother at Triyugi Narayan Temple in the state of Uttarakhand in India.

> **The state of Uttarakhand has been known from time immemorial as the Daiva Bhumi (abode of the angels) - a link between the Heaven and the Earth, with several sites of spiritual significance; Haridwar being known as the Stairway to Heaven (the access door to God).**

Thus, the marriage of God Shiva with Parvati (an elevated mortal human) was an example indicating how a mortal soul could merge with God, and thereby establishing the concept of 'Ardha-Narishwar' (the union of two souls to become one soul resulting in the birth of a subtle new born called God-Child).

The 'Sanatan Dharma' concepts of how a mortal human can achieve liberation to merge with God has been experienced by a number of real-life humans, such as Goddess

Parvati uniting with Lord Shiva, Mirabai merging with Lord Krishna, Baijnath, a devout devotee of Lord Shiva (at Palampur in Himachal Pradesh), Tarkeshwar at Lansdowne in Garhwal district of Uttarakhand, and hundreds of others. They all took different paths to achieve their salvation and to merge with God.

Ved and Malti's path to achieve salvation was an unique way by way of achieving perfection via the concept of 'Ardh-Narishwar' – a state that could be achieved via the institution of marriage.

Ved and Malti's journey ended, when their seventh consecutive marriage in seven lifetimes was conducted at the same site at Triyugi Narayan Temple, Gupt Kashi.

Seven lifetimes of marriage to the same partner, is like graduating from one class to a higher class of acquiring knowledge about the opposite 'principle' and perfecting the self from a lower level of consciousness to a higher level of consciousness.

Ved and Malti, were ordained as the Twin-Flames, as they qualified to become eternal soul-mates after achieving the state of Ardha-Narishwar – both acquiring equality with each other in terms of their 'Purush', and 'Prakriti' – the wisdom of creation, and the power of nature – the creation – a perfect blend of fifty percent male, fifty percent female gender centric consciousness.

It is believed that Lord Shiva, and Lord Vishnu personally blessed those who got married at Gupt Kashi, or at Triyugi Narayan.

The trend of solemnizing a marriage at Gupt Kashi still continues till present day. Recently the author witnessed an entourage of about 30 people who came down from the USA for solemnizing such a marriage at Gupt Kashi.

The 35-year-old Bride was a lawyer of Indian origin from New Jersey, a devotee of Lord Shiva, and the 40 year old American Groom, also from the same place, got their wishes fulfilled in a grand marriage ceremony conducted at Gupt Kashi.

Needless to say, that the overwhelming empowering effect of their marriage ceremony itself at Gupt Kashi provided the flame of their marriage going bright every passing day.

And it was not surprising that both Ved and Malti were guided in their dream to come to Gupt Kashi. The dream showed that Ved and Malti were welcomed by the villagers of Gupt Kashi in a grand reception.

There were two camps amongst the villagers. One camp who claimed to be the groom's party, took Ved to their own campus, and the other camp who claimed to be the bride's party took them to their own campus at a different location of the village. The tradition has it that both the camps hold a number of rituals involving the bride and the groom prior to the actual marriage preparing them with numerous protocols and wisdom for their conjugal married life.

These rituals continue for about two weeks till the actual marriage ceremony as per the protocols of all Hindu marriages.

These rituals are revered by all as the foundation of God's covenant of a marriage.

The two weeks of celebrations for the Twin-Flame involving the villagers was a rare and 'once in a lifetime' opportunity for the villagers, and the villagers took great pride in it as they believed that they too were the chosen ones for being a part of such a heavenly event. The festivity in the village included endless community feasting and dancing, Kirtans (mass singing of religious rhymes), Sangeet (musical event portrayal of a marriage), Haldi Ceremony (a ritual of body anointing with Haldi - Turmeric), Mehendi Ceremony (drawing beautiful tattoo designs on the palms of the hand and arms with Henna paste), ring ceremony, and the grooms party visiting the bride with gifts for the bride - best of jewelry and dresses, the bride's party providing all house hold furnishings and kitchen equipment for their future life for the bride and the groom, and so on.

The final ritual of the marriage ceremony took place at the temple after two weeks of orientation prior to the actual ceremony.

The actual marriage is a daylong spiritual event starting in the morning and ending late in the afternoon with a common feast for all the villagers and guests, attending the event from faraway places.

Needless to say, that it's an event right out of God's endless bounty of 'Leela' – an act of mysterious spiritual fervor.

Their dream also showed Mahavatar Babaji, and the Mountain Man around the fire pit along with several unfamiliar faces throwing flowers and petals at them during the marriage ceremony.

The connotations of the dream were not lost on them as they felt that they were now upgraded to a superior realm of consciousness, to be accepted by the divinity as one united soul - a God-Child.

The Journey To Gupt Kashi:

They departed from Jageswar Dham at Almora, and once again headed towards Kedarnath on their way to Gupt Kashi.

Gupt Kashi was about 25 Km from Kedarnath, a difficult place to reach.

When they reached the highly revered Triyugi Narayan village at the confluence of the legendary Mandakini River and the Sone Ganga River, a series of baffling incidents welcomed them.

The first one was when an aggressive Fakir with long gray beard and knotted unkempt hair greeted them with a volley of expletives.

He looked like a regular Himalayan Sadhu, but he didn't behave like one. He questioned Ved and Malti the purpose of their visit to Triyugi Narayan Village, and warned them not to make the same mistake of getting married like many others who believed that marriage was a divine thing. Few villagers came and gathered around them hearing the commotion caused by the 'Naastik Baba' – as he was known in this region.

The word Naastik means – a non-believer; exactly the opposite of the word 'Aastik', which means a believer of God's providence.

A few villagers came to their rescue and took them away from Nastik Baba, and guided them to their village temple to do the 'Atithee-Sanskar' (the practice of welcoming a guest and showing respect).

And once they freshened up and served with some tea and snacks, the villagers asked them the purpose of their visit.

Ved clarified that they were wandering monks and were on their way to Gupt Kashi to experience the vibrations of the 'Ardh-Narishwar' – the half male-half female Avatar of Shiva and Parvati.

On hearing that they were monks, the villagers became more respectful towards them and brought some packed eatables for them to carry during their journey.

And just as they were getting ready to resume their journey, an old man with a slight hump rushed to them. He seemed very excited to see Ved and Malti. He knelt down at their feet and started weeping uncontrollably. They were taken aback seeing this elderly man whom they had never seen before and weeping at their feet.

"I have been waiting for such a long time for you to come, and almost gave up!" the old man spoke amidst his sobbing. "But Babaji finally answered my prayers. And now that you have come, you have given me the opportunity to serve you once again to carry out my vows." The villagers who were quite familiar with the old man and considered him to be just another one of those senile 'wanna-be' fakirs, were amused seeing his theatrics and watched on.

Ved lifted the old man from his kneeling position and hugged him passionately.

"Your place is not at my feet," Ved said. "You are held in high esteem in my heart, and you were never indebted to me."

Now it was Malti's turn to be bewildered seeing Ved hug the old man, and asked, "Do you know him, Ved?"

"Yes Malti, don't you remember him?" Ved asked.

Suddenly in a flash, Malti remembered – he was Manu Baba, their home-priest whose family had served Ved's family for many generations.

Ved remembered the incident when he had rescued Manu from being swept away during the flood when they were young. Manu's parents were swept away in the flood, but Manu was rescued by Ved, risking his own life. Ved was given a hero's welcome by the villagers for his selfless act and was rewarded by the village council for his act of bravery.

Malti suddenly realized that these were memories from their previous life, and also that Ved was her husband in that life too!

A shiver ran through her body, and in a daze, she blurted out, "But Ved, wasn't that in our previous birth?"

"Yes," Ved replied, "You were Malini then, and I was Shashank."

The realization that they were Twin-Flames sunk in deeper in her mind and Manu was a living proof.

The realization that they were arriving at Gupt Kashi very soon sent a shiver of apprehension through her consciousness.

Malti's reverie broke as Ved asked her, "Don't you remember Manu, our Manu Baba? He conducted our marriage ceremony at this very place in Triyugi Narayan!"

Malti nodded her head in silence and looked at Manu in awe!

They remembered how Manu had become very spiritual, and having remained a bachelor all his life, had spent a lot of time meditating and led a life of Bairagya (abstinence from familial bondage). He became a well-known priest and a highly skilled astrologer with amazing intuitive powers. He was an invaluable asset for the society.

And they also remembered how one day they had found him dead in sitting position, deep in meditation. It was an unbearable loss for Ved, and he never seemed to recover from the shock. He became a recluse until one night Manu came in his dreams and promised that he will once again come to conduct their marriage at Gupt Kashi in his next life. The villagers who were mute spectators all this while suddenly realized that something strange was happening right in front of their eyes!

They quietly listened to Ved and Malti discussing about their past life, and one of them couldn't resist himself from asking as to what was going on.

But Ved didn't want to get entangled in any further discussion with the villagers, and walked away with Malti and Manu, after thanking them for their hospitality.

The three of them resumed their trek towards Gupt Kashi in silence, immersed deep in their own thoughts.

They looked at Manu with side glances from time to time wondering as to what was going on in his mind, and what all things that must have happened in his present life.

Manu seemed to read their thoughts and spoke, "I was born in a poor family at Tungnath - the highest location of a Shiva temple in the world.

"My father once again, was a temple priest. But instead of taking over the job of my father after he passed away, I travelled in the Himalayas seeking salvation.

"That's when Mahavatar Babaji gave me his Darshan (face to face appearance), and I came to know about the future course of my life. He said that you two will come again, and that I will have the privilege to conduct your marriage ceremony once again at the same site at Triyugi Narayan Temple where I had conducted your marriage in our previous life.

"This marriage – a rare and precious union of a Twin-Flame at this same pious place where Lord Brahma conducted the marriage ceremony of Shiva and Parvati, augers well for the future of humanity, and will also release me from the cycle of birth- after being the chosen one for conducting this rare marriage ceremony of a Twin-Flame for two successive lifetimes!"

Manu paused for a while, and looked up saying, "Now you know how important it was for me waiting for you two to show up?"

They nodded in silence, and Ved said, "We are the 'blessed-ones' here Manu, to be guided to come here by Mahavatar Babaji to once again get united with you.

"All this couldn't have been possible without your presence Manu, and we shall forever remain deeply indebted to you." Manu shook his head and said, "On the contrary, I have been privileged to be assigned this divine task of reuniting a twin-flame for the second successive time at this sacred venue, and that's a rare feat, isn't it?"

Ved thanked Mahavatar Babaji silently in his mind for letting him know in advance in his dream about his impending marriage reunion.

The distance of about 38 Kms between Triyugi Narayan and Gupt Kashi was covered in three and a half hours of walking on the hilly terrain, and they reached their destination towards the late afternoon.

They were welcomed at Gupt Kashi by an elderly couple known to Manu.

Manu left Ved and Malti with their host and promised to return the next morning.

Their host looked after them with utmost respect as per the traditions of Indian culture, where guests are equated with God.

Manu returned the next morning with the news that a very auspicious 'muhurat' (auspicious time as per the astrological configurations) was found after two weeks for their reunion marriage at the premises of the Triyugi Narayan temple.

He quickly left once again, saying that he had a lot of arrangements to make for the marriage, and also alert the villagers with details of protocols and preparation.

Ved and Malti had two weeks in hand which they decided to spend on visiting the temples of Lord Shiva and Lord Vishnu – to take their blessings, and also to thank them for their grace and to seek their presence during the auspicious moment of their reunion marriage.

But a big surprise awaited them on the very next day when two groups of people approached them, and amidst a lot of celebratory singing and dancing took Ved and Malti to two different camps – one group representing the groom's side, and the other representing the bride's side.

It was made abundantly clear to them that from now on Ved and Malti would not be allowed to see each other till the time of their marriage at the temple.

The next two weeks were spent in the camps holding numerous rituals and orientation program about the covenants of a Hindu marriage on a much higher plane as per Vedic wisdom and sciences. It was same as described to them by the Mountain Man at the Valley of Flowers, and things were happening exactly in the same way.

Ved and Malti were visited every day by hundreds of people at their respective camps who thronged to take their blessings as this was an event of divinity like no other.

Both the camps received gifts and donation from the villagers and also those who came to visit from distant places.

It is also believed that Devas, and Devtas (Gods, and Angels) descend during such occasions to bless the twin-flame couple – the union marriage being considered as a recognition of the fact that a new God-Child was about to be born.

The Marriage :-

Their reunion marriage took place exactly as Ved had dreamt. The resonance of the vibrations of the drums and the Vedic mantras created waves of pulsation over the dancing flames of the Havan Fire that leapt into the sky.

Ved and Malti could clearly see Mahavatar Babaji and the Mountain Man amidst hundreds of others throwing flowers and petals at them in a show of acknowledgement of their reunion marriage and showering them with blessings.

Manu's joy and pride was seen to be believed, as he chanted the Vedic mantras while conducting the marriage rituals.

Ved and Malti were pleasantly surprised to see a group of 10-12 foreigners including Yukta and Yamini, who came down and arrived at Gupt Kashi for their marriage. They were quite amused to see that Yukta and Yamini fervently describing the traditions of a Hindu marriage to the foreigners, and about the concepts of the mother of all marriages – the 'Ardha-Narishwar' twin flame ceremony which was considered to be a celestial affair.

The divine ceremony continued for well over six hours of Vedic mantra chanting, several vows and rituals of dedicating and surrendering to God, and tying the marital knot etc.

Finally, the time came for the final moment - the manifestation of Ardha-Narishwar – the blending of the soul mates into oneness.

This was a breath-taking moment when an inter-play of 'Bhoutic', and 'Incorporeal' (physical and metaphysical) was about to be witnessed by the thousands assembled at the temple compound of Triyugi Narayan.

In normal Hindu marriages the couple had to take the 'Saat-Pheras' (walking seven rounds around the fire), for marriage vows taken for seven-life times of soul-mate companionship.

But this Twin-Flame ceremony, being the eighth time of togetherness, the couple now had attained a state of elevated soul-mate status, and hence the process for the occasion was different, and gained a celestial acknowledgement.

And just when the crescendo of the Havan – the fire ritual, and the chanting of Mantras were coming to an end, a never seen before spectacle unfolded.

The guests witnessed an astonishing sight right in front of their eyes.

A blinding million watts of illumination began to engulf the area surrounding the Havan fire and it began to lift upward. It kept on moving upward and finally floated at the top of the temple dome. The top of the temple dome seemed to have parted up and a huge ball of dazzling light stood floating atop the temple dome in the open sky.

It took quite a while before the guests could look at the spectacle in front of their eyes. But gradually their eyes were able to bear the brightness and what they saw next was beyond any form of human comprehension.

The people observing the spectacle lost all sense of their consciousness as they saw Ved and Malti sat facing each other amidst the bright dazzle of illumination in an intent state of meditation.

Brilliant waves of rays emerged from their third eye - like laser beams, and the rays collided at a midpoint between each other, creating an explosion of multi-colored fusion.

This interplay of light and sound seemingly went on for eternity for the onlookers, although it was only for a few seconds.

And as the bandwidth of the waves emerging from their third eye grew bigger and bigger, the distance between them shrank, and they began to move towards each other as if being sucked inward into the whirlpool of the fusion of light. This continued till their bodies merged into the whirlpool, and both Ved and Malti merged into each other!

The viewers could no longer see their physical contours anymore and all they could see was one single bright glow of illumination. The sound of conch shells blown by hundreds of priests drowned the air. The air was filled with the floral petals and fragrance of the Eden.

Gradually all the cacophony of light and sound ceased as the newly formed glow moved upward slowly disappearing into the sky.

Then a numbing silence engulfed the space, and suddenly the guests were brought back to their senses, as if awakening after a dream.

All they could see and feel now was that they were just waking up from a prolonged sleep, feeling a little drowsy and yet fresh.

Slowly the truth sunk in, that they had just witnessed something that happened at a much higher plane of consciousness where Ved and Malti had merged into oneness.

They could not comprehend much as to what had really transpired after the bright dazzling light had appeared.

And to their utter sense of horror, they realized that they had no memory of anything beyond that.

And then after some time, they again saw Ved, Malti, and Manu Baba sitting quietly in the same spot where they had been sitting earlier!

That's when, much to everyone's relief, Manu Baba, the chief priest conducting the Ardh-Nariswar marriage ceremony stood up in front of them to explain to them as to what had really transpired and thanked them for their participation in this divine event.

And then Manu Baba declared that the ceremony was over, and all the guests at the ceremony were led to a hall for the feast.

The system was that the guests would sit in rows on the floor and a multi-course meal would be served by the 'Sevaks' (volunteers who served the food). The food was served on banana leaves, and water was served in earthen glasses.

The guests could start eating only after the married couple would address the guests with a prayer requesting all the guests to accept the food as an acknowledgement of the host's prayers for their blessings.

The protocol in all temple-related social ceremonies was that a trained kitchen staff from the temple's management would cook and serve the food as 'Prasad' – food offerings to God.

And then it was time for the Bride camp to do the formal rituals of bidding goodbye to the Bride (a chariot ride for the Bride to the Groom's camp), and for the Groom's camp to welcome the Bride into their camp, and then together depart from the marriage campus for the Groom's home.

The departure ceremony of the Bride to the Groom's house was an emotionally charged moment with lots of crying and weeping as their beloved daughter was being taken away by the Groom.

Ved and Malti were then taken to a specially decorated house that was prepared for the married couple to spend the night at 'Phool-Sajya' (a bedroom specially decorated with flowers and perfumes for their honeymoon night).

Thus, the milestone moment in their lives manifested exactly as was predicted by the Mountain Man.

Ved and Malti stayed for a few more days at Gupt Kashi as per the protocols for thanksgiving, and then it was time for them to move on into the next phase of their life.

They requested Manu to accompany them from then on, in their journey as travelling monks.

Manu readily agreed to do that, and it was all very hunky-dory once again like in their previous life.

***

Chapter IV

VEDIC COVENANT OF MARRIAGE

The manifestation of the 'Ardha- Narishwar' – the 'half male-half female' avatar of Lord Shiva, and his spouse Goddess Parvati at the divine matrimonial site Gupt-Kashi is a significant portrayal of the purpose of two souls of the opposite sex entering into an institution of marriage.

When a male and a female ties up into the bond of a marriage, what they actually do is to sign up into a commitment of merging into each other at their soul level to become one – with an intent to attain perfection in terms of becoming equal in their level of consciousness of their awareness of maleness and femaleness - literally a state beyond being a male and a female.

According to Vedic wisdom it is also believed that any married couple who remain a couple for seven consecutive lifetimes, can evolve to a level called Twin-Flame and they can further evolve to a state of oneness, and thus graduating to the plane of angels.

In Hinduism, the plane at which the soul dwells are calibrated like this – 'Atman' (an ordinary human soul), 'Mahan Atman' (a superior human soul), 'Devaatma' (an angelic soul), and beyond that is 'Parmaatma' (the supreme divine soul of God consciousness).

The Twin-Flame concept rides on the Vedic concept that broadly outlines and describes the covenants of a marriage as one of the basic foundations upon which stood the entire creation of God, the SAMSARA – our planetary-eco system.

Marriage is a gift-wrapped package from God – a fabric that stitched together the entire fundamental structure of his entire creation, and an autonomous process of procreation and renewal.

Marriage by itself is a journey of awakening for both the partners - a roller-coaster journey with several ups and downs and many a tumultuous 'pressure-cooker' moments that exposes the short-comings of the two individuals which are needed to be overcome by them.

When the couple learns to tide over numerous situations that life throws at them, their bond becomes stronger and their faith and trust in each other flourishes.

Call it maturity or call it becoming wiser, in either case they graduate to a higher level of unitedness.

A mother and a father are created out of the marriage.

The mother – an epitome of limitless unconditional love and sacrifice, and a father who nurtures, protects, and provides the family at an unprecedented level of self-less sacrifice, is one of the nectars of Godliness churned out from the institution of a marriage.

There is no relationship on earth that is more powerful than the 'Mother-Child' relationship; and there is no symbolic-representation of God on Earth as that of a father- as the protector and the provider, and the look-up to figure- just as we do to God.

What parents are to their children, is God to his entire creation.

A marriage not only unites two individuals, but an additional perk from a marriage is the bonding between the families of the couple, that enhances a social bonding at a broader level.

From this high-value family bonding, one can learn the unconditional nature of 'Dharma' (responsibility) in a similar manner in which God did for his entire creation.

The vows taken in those auspicious moments of saying "I Do" are often drowned immediately thereafter in the euphoria of the celebrations. No one cares what vows were taken. It's only when two different mindsets share their lives, two sets of thought process come to the surface, that the couple learns to accept each other. Those who learn to respect each other and bend a little to accept the other, their love and trust in each other grow, and the marriage blossoms.

It's a pity, the opposite is the case in present times when up to 40-50% of the marriages, they end up in divorce.

A marriage by itself opens up quite a few doors that supplement the sustenance of the human-eco system.

When the couple settles down learning to share each other's life, their egos begin to surface, followed by the integrated adaptation of the persona between the two individuals.

Some adapt easily and click as a team, while many others are not that fortunate.

To accommodate another person in one's life, one needs an attitude of acceptance, and that does not happen easily.

What makes a marriage tick, and what gives way to a break-up depends upon one's personal dedication and belief in the self.

Does a break-up really solve the issues that caused the break-up?

In most cases it doesn't, except in some cases bordering on physical abuse and intentional superiority complex.

It is also seen that some separation happens due to lack of compatibility and intellect.

Some break-ups also happened due to a spur of the moment ego-centric decision- a phenomenon in which the person decides that enough is enough, only to repent such a decision later with a lingering doubt in the mind. Yet, people move on in life, and repeat the same mistake over and over again, learning the hard way to become wiser later, having learnt from past mistakes.

Marriage unilaterally demands sacrifice at all levels for the greater good, and it's not just about petty issues with promise for a healthy relationship – there has to be devotion and respect for it to move forward.

Remembering to honour the vows that were taken at the time of the entering into the bond of marriage for learning about the 'whys' and the 'hows' to remain true to those vows, could make all the difference in the sustenance of a marriage.

Ancient Vedic wisdom in Hinduism explains the scientific purpose behind the covenant of marriage, and how facing-off the storms of a married life can result in the fulfillment of the real purpose as to why the institution of a marriage was created.

The history of how the marriage vows came into practice goes back to the 16th century, as mentioned in the 'Book of Common Prayers' in Christianity.

Yet, there are records dating back to the 11th century 'Sarum' - a Latin liturgical form used in English Church even before the Book of Common Prayers.

It goes back even further in ancient Indian culture as mentioned in the Vedas and Upanishads.

The vows themselves have been accepted as expressions of God, but written in word by the keepers of faith in accordance with compliance along the religious scriptures.

Hence every religion expresses these vows as per their own ethical code of social conduct.

It's not the formatted words of commitment that the priest conducting the marriage ceremony make the couple utter before the couple seals the commitment of matrimony by exchanging the rings that is of much of a significance in the holistic perspective of things, it's the overall perspective of the institution of marriage that is of importance – as to what the whole concept of the union of the two individuals of the opposite sex signify.

As it is rightly called as the 'Institution of Marriage' in which it's not about the two persons alone, who enter into a contract to share their lives and to procreate children to make a family – the whole attendees too become responsible about the process.

So, what is the larger picture here?

The larger picture can be illustrated in the following manner –

- Primarily, marriage is the only means to sustenance of the human-eco system: the life and death syndrome,

otherwise humanity will cease to exist after a period of time.
- The union of two individuals in the bondage of marriage is considered to be an act of divinity for a far greater purpose, contrary to what the married couples might think.
- It is often said that marriages are made in heaven, just as they also say that births and deaths are decided in heaven. Hence there is definitely a bigger game plan here.
- Marriage teaches the couple, the concepts of acceptance and adaptability to support each other in the best, or in the worst of times, which in turn is a process of evolution for the two individuals to a higher self.
- A marriage empowers the value of trust and faith, to experience the purity of a relationship.
- A marriage manifests into a family and that creates more relationships.
- The algorithm of family and relationships manifest into an entire human-eco system.
- Most importantly, marriage brings in added values of bonding and promotes community living, which is unique by itself.
- From out of a marriage, is born the strongest bonding that of a mother and child relationship on one dimension, and also the relationship of unparalleled significance that of the father.
- The concept of unconditional and self-less love is born out of such 'parent-child' relationship.
- Every father and a mother experience this concept of unconditional and self-less love, and sacrifice – a new

expression of life that they were not aware of earlier.

- Going into a full circle, the two individuals, after having experienced the institution of marriage, evolve into a more mature version of the self, and is able to share their concept of unconditional love to others outside the parameters of their family as well, by accepting others as they are and adapting to others the same way they did with their partner when they started their married life.
- It further leads to a much larger game plan – that of spirituality that teaches us how to shelve the ego and discover the identity of one's true self and nature.
- Last, but not the least, as was described in the previous chapter – marriage can lead to the unification of the two souls to such a higher plane so that a 'God-Child' is born.

Thus, as we see, the institution of marriage is a big master plan of God that encompasses a much bigger holistic objective.

The vows are just the means to enforce discipline in them for keeping the marriage intact, and to teach them the basic responsibilities to shoulder.

***

Chapter V

DEV BHOOMI – THE HIMALAYAS

An experience of the Gross-Physical, and the Meta- Cosmic

After spending a few more days in Gupt Kashi after their 'Twin-Flame' reunion marriage and having visited all the five 'Avatars' of Lord Shiva (Panch Kashi), and also the temples of Lord Vishnu to show their gratitude, Ved and Malti headed for the Kailash Man-Sarovar pilgrimage at Mount Kailash as a prelude to their visit to the famous Kumbh Mela, held at the confluence of the three rivers - the Ganges, the Yamuna, and river Saraswati (no longer in existence) at Prayagraj (city of Allahabad in India).

Mount Kailash, in the Himalayan mountain range, and the equally mysterious secrets of the 'Kumbh Mela' (the largest spiritual fair with about eighty million footfalls) is held every twelve years in India, and are two of the most intriguing events that has baffled the best of the scientific minds.

Dev Bhoomi Himalaya, and Kaliash Parvat (Mount Kailash):

The word Himalaya which literally means 'Snow World' is spread across about 2500 Kms from the northern part of India across Nepal, China, Tibet, Bhutan, and up to the eastern most state of Arunachal Pradesh in India.

What is more special about the Himalayas is that it is also the universal home to seekers of the truth, and spirituality. Many westerners frustrated with the neo-capitalistic mindset come to this region seeking answers to fill the voids in their mind.

Amidst the unparalleled beauty and grandeur of the Himalayan range, stands the majestic Kailash Parvat (Mt. Kailash), a stronghold bed of Yogic wisdom and spirituality since time immemorial.

The mystique of the Kailash Parvat has captivated the curiosity of all – the saints and the sadhus, the historians and the anthropologists, the climbers, the movie makers and journalists etc.

Around the basic concept of the main pilgrimage to the Kailash Mansarovar, there are also five other Kailash pilgrimages sites spread across Tibet(1), Himachal Pradesh(3), and Uttarakhand(1) in India. They are – Kailash Mansarovar in Tibet, Adi Kailash in Uttarakhand, and the rest of the three – Mani Mahesh, Kinnaur Kailash, and Shrikhand Mahadev in Himachal Pradesh.

Himalayan pilgrimage centers have always been associated with tough trekking across highly dangerous hills, and pilgrimage to Panch Kailash sets the bar like no other.

Shrikhand Mahadev is the most perilous trek where a number of visitors die every year. The trek to the Kailash Mansarovar too is quite a difficult one.

But no matter how tough the treks are, the devotees always claim that all their tiredness is forgotten once they reach their destination due to the high level of divine energies prevalent there, and their overwhelming devotion gives them a Daivik (angelic) experience.

The freezing cold, the low oxygen level at those high altitude and lack of normal facilities don't matter anymore to those thousands of believers - 'Aastiks'.

It's an oasis and a paradise where humans find answers to questions no religion could ever offer, regardless of their faith or belief - like in an open university for the entire humanity.

The Himalayan Dev Bhoomi is an open university of the most unconventional nature suitable only for the genuine students of spirituality who are ready to relinquish all forms of worldly attachments to unravel the absolute truth about God.

Finding God is not a possibility, but experiencing God is inevitable if one walks the path of spirituality. And all the paths lead to the Himalayas where the lessons are learnt at a higher plane of perception for the realization of God.

The unique place near the Mansarovar at the foot of the Mt.Kailash, or the Kailash Parvat, the abode of Lord Shiva known as the 'Siddhashram', and popularly known as the Gyanjganj, is believed to be the ultimate Ashrama – the school, college, or university whatever one chooses to call it, to qualify to elevate the self from a lower self to enlightenment and self-liberation.

Thus, Gyanganj is also referred to as the gateway to heaven, or the door to salvation.

Gyanganj can be accessed only by those with elevated levels of consciousness, and not by ordinary beings, as it is believed to exist at a higher plane of perception.

The mystique energies and the vibrations prevailing around Gyanganj inspired thousands of 'Aastikas' (believers) to seek and achieve Nirvana over thousands of years, and still continue to do so even today.

The rich ancient tradition of Himalayan spirituality is still as vibrant today as it has been thousands of years ago and shall remain so till eternity.

The masters and the sadhus who lived there travelled across the region, leaving in their trail the wisdom of the Gods and the truths that no religious book or faith could ever teach.

Most of the Himalayan region lies at heights of 15,000 to 25,000 feet with very thin air with low oxygen, and are not easily accessible to normal pilgrims or tourists.

Yet these are the places where the masters and sadhus of the Himalayan school of spirituality pursued and taught their wisdom at. Here, the seekers learnt to be fully surrendered in the lap of nature, and in turn nature nurtured them in a motherly manner – a form of poetry that can at best be described as the theme of love, and in a most unconditional manner.

The nomadic style of the Himalayan sadhus and monks are like mobile schools sowing the seeds of spirituality and imparting wisdom in the minds of the people whoever sought to learn from them.

And in return the people provided these sadhus with food and provision.

The sadhus and monks are highly revered by the villagers who lived nearby, and are treated as if they were direct messengers of God.

Once when Ved, Malti, and Manu forayed into one such village at a remote isolated region deep in the Himalayas, they learnt that the villagers have not had the honor to host a single sadhu for the last three months, and they felt it was a bad omen for them, and an indication that something bad was going to happen to them.

And when Ved, Malti, and Manu appeared in their village they greeted them with great happiness, devotion and honor.

They made them sit on wooden 'peeta' stools, washed their feet, and applied oil to their tired feet. Then they took them inside their hut and fed them with fruits and 'Payasam' (sweetened rice dish cooked in milk) and sweets.

Then they arranged 'Khatiyas' (wooden cot/bed made of knitted jute ropes) for them to rest.

The villagers took turns to provide them hospitality and wouldn't let them leave.

They enjoyed their hospitality for 3-4 days and they too reciprocated by teaching the villagers ways to improve their lifestyle, health and wellness, and ways to improve their earning by modern ways of crop cultivation, and making the best use of their resources.

Ved, Malti, and Manu too learnt a few things from these villagers, and some invaluable wisdom that were imparted to them by other visiting sadhus and monks as well.

And it was with a heavy heart that the villagers bade them farewell, requesting them to visit again.

Wandering around Himalayan region brought a profound change in Ved and Malti's mental attitude and their thinking pattern. Now they acquired a much more expanded vision while interpreting things.

Ved, Malti, and Manu gradually acclimatized themselves to the climatic conditions, and the characteristics of glacial behavior.

They learnt to become themselves a part of the sudden avalanches, blizzards and storms, and other dangers of the snowy world of the Himalayas, by reading the signs and signals with their intuitive intellect.

They no longer planned things in advance and were open to any kind of situation that confronted them. Fear was the last thing that they thought of anymore.

They would frequently meet other sadhus of the region who treated them with utmost kindness and camaraderie, by exchanging spiritual wisdom and unique techniques of Yogic procedures, and ways of harnessing life force energies from the Sun.

Just by being there and wandering around the seemingly innocuous nature of the Himalayan region, taught Ved, Malti, and Manu things that they could never have learnt elsewhere. And one thing that they learnt now was not to keep any expectations, and to accept things as they were.

Solitude, and interacting with the subtle changing nuances of the energies of the day – during the morning, noon, and in the evening twilight, taught them a new kind of a language all together - a language that all the wandering sadhus and monks were adept at.

Not many words were exchanged, and few that were spoken, were not words from our common vocabulary – these words originated from out of the perceptions of their natural habitat. Some sounds, some syllables, or some expressions.

The hissing sounds of the icy winds, the gushing sounds of the waters of the streams, and the distant sound of flute played by the shepherds and cow tenders felt like as if the nature was performing an orchestra of its own!

The hardship and having to go without food for days were of no concern to them anymore and they became one with the nature, and were nurtured by Mother Nature herself.

During these wandering days Ved, Malti, and Manu had their fair share of miracles and paranormal experiences too.

Once, they were caught in a sudden blizzard and they found themselves slowly being buried in a quickly forming gorge. They felt that well, this was it – an end to an ignominious errand in their spiritual pursuit in the Himalayas.

But just as the blanket of snow covered them completely, they began to feel some warmth emanating from around them. They couldn't make out what it was, but realized that they were being sheltered by two huge mountain bears. The warmth emanated was from the furry Himalayan bears!

They lay in the gorge sheltered by the bears till the dawn of the next day, and the bears took them out from the gorge, and into a bright sunny morning. The bears took them to a nearby village and then they left them on their own.

When the villagers found them, they were in a deep state of exhaustion and fatigue. The villagers nursed them back over the next few days and provided them with food, and shelter.

When later Ved narrated the incident to the villagers they were awestruck and said that they were familiar with the story of the two bears.

Now it was their turn to be awestruck and asked the villagers as to what the story was.

The villagers said that the two bears were a pair of male and female bears who lived with a legendary Himalayan sadhu who was believed to have lived for more than a hundred and ninety years. And after the sadhu took his Maha Samadhi, the two bears lived around the region and helped people in distress. It was also believed that the sadhu had blessed the bears before he took his Maha Samadhi with immortality, and to protect those who were in peril.

Numerous such fables floated around in the playground of the Himalayan school of spiritualism.

The Dev Bhoomi of the Himalayas has numerous facets of mystic wisdom that can never be explored and discovered by any one single individual.

Each seeker stumbled upon something or the other, and the profoundness of that much of wisdom was enough for them to achieve their enlightenment.

Thus, many of these self-realized sadhus get be known by their unique names, such as Bangali Baba, Neem Karoli Baba, Pilot Baba, Tiger Baba, and many such.

Just like the individuals, there are also a brand of sadhus who got their names because of their style and discipline of spiritualism:

Naga Sadhus:

The Naga Sadhus are a brand of sadhus known to attract the curiosity of the common people during the Kumbh Mela due to their nakedness (nanga -mans naked), and for their prowess for executing extremely severe penances, and staying naked, smudged with ashes on their bodies even in the coldest of places in the Himalayan belt.

The lineage of the Naga Sadhus goes back right up to the very start of human civilization. They lived in 'Akharas' (units/camps), and generally are seen only during the Kumbh Meal at Prayagraj, city of Allahabad in India.

Aghori –

This is another brand of sadhus well known for their extremely unusual style of behavior bordering on complete disdain for normal forms of lifestyle. Their strength was complete surrendered devotion to Lord Shiva, who is also considered to remain smudged in ashes of the cremation grounds and spending more time with the dead.

That is the reason that Lord Shiva is associated with the concept of death and beyond. The Aghoris try to imitate this form of concept for attainment of Moksha - from 'Shava' (dead body) to 'Shiva' (immortality).

Thus, the Aghoris spend time meditating at the cremation grounds, bathing in the ashes and devouring the flesh, and dancing in ecstasy.

Though this may sound barbaric, there is much deeper depth to their tradition than is understood by a common mind. Their pursuit is known as 'Oghora-path' – the path of the Aghoris.

Vaishnava Sadhus:

These are yet another brand of sadhus (sanyasi) who follow the path of Vishnu Bhakti (followers of Lord Vishnu, one of the Hindu trinity of Gods).

And most unlike the Naga Sadhus, and Aghori Sadhus, the Vaishnava Sadhus prefer to keep themselves clean and many of them keep a clean-shaven head with a lock of hair at the back of the head like a pony tail, eg. Mahaprabhu Chaitanya Maharaj, the ISKON followers (devotees of Lord Krishna), and Sudama etc.

What is common to all these brands of ascetics is that they all are extremely poor, and they neither have the means of earning, and nor do they have any possession, or a regular place to stay.

For them living in acute poverty is a means to their God-connect.

They survive on the 'Viksha' – fruits, and other food and provisions offered by people who revere their austerity.

One common message they all portray is that nothing in life is permanent and imperishable, and hence divinity is the only refuge that matters.

Their lifestyle is a portrayal of how to not be fooled by the lures of 'Maya' (illusion), greed, and all the other forms of bondage that humans are subject to in 'Samsara' – life in the human eco system. Not much is talked about the presence of the paranormal amidst our Samsara (the human eco-system), but the reality is that our entire human eco system is governed by the unseen hands of a superior intelligence.

Mount Kailash, the abode of Lord Shiva – one of the Trinity of Hindu Gods– which is also believed to be the epicenter of our planet earth, is a prime example.

The 'HIRANYA-GARBHA', as mentioned in the Rig Veda, from which manifested the universe, and the 'Kamandal' from which 'Life' flowed, is attributed to Lord Shiva's presence at the geometrically perfect Mt.Kailash peak, and which has been recorded time and again over thousands of years by spiritual monks, as well as explorers and scientists. It has been verified by researchers that numerous paranormal facets prevail at the Mt. Kailash, such as - an abnormal electro-magnetic energy field, time-leap, and space, vibrations of the emanating sound of 'AUM', and many such others.

Nobody ever has succeeded in climbing the peak is as surreal as it gets.

One ages at a rapid pace (verified by Russian climbers who died a premature death due to ageing quickly while trying to climb the Mt.Kailash peak).

While we humans perform at a lower plane of knowledge and wisdom, a superior intelligence prevailing at a higher plane is active in the governance of the planetary system – such as, the management of the astrological configurations of the universe, the seasons, the oceans, the oxygen, the balance of nature and the perfect levels of cosmic energies, etc. to name only a few.

The superior intelligence (divinity) involved in the management of the universe that manages the eco-system, and the life form on our planet is not a subject that our scientists and also our own gross material minds know much of about!

The astrophysicists and astrologers do make their calculations, but they appear to be completely ignorant about their 'whys', and the 'hows' of it.

The ancient mathematical and geo-astral sciences that are far advanced than our modern sciences function seamlessly towards the management and sustenance of our planetary eco system.

Our ancient Rishis calculated the distances between the earth and other planets thousands of years accurately to the last decimal, which our scientists have been able to only recently.

The Mt.Kailash, aka the Kailash Parvat as it is called in India, is said to be the epicenter for channelizing the geo-physical management of our planet. It also happens to be a highly revered and sacred pilgrimage of the Hindu religion, and the 'Himalayan tradition' of spiritualism thrives in this region over thousands of years.

A general belief system is that the Mt.Kailash is the connection between the heaven and Earth as the point of cosmic confluence.

Manu took Ved and Malti to the Kailash Mansarovar – a lake at the base of the Mount Kailash where the devotees bathe to purify themselves before they proceed for the circumambulation (walk clockwise) of the mountain as a part of their pilgrimage.

There are two lakes there – Kailash Mansarovar, shaped like the Sun is for the angels, and the Rakshastal, shaped like the crescent is for the demons.

The Sun shaped Mansarovar lake signifies all that is bright and positive, while the crescent shaped lake, the Rakshastal represents negativity and darkness.

Yet both are an integral part of the whole pilgrimage.

There is no reference to any God here as such, neither Hindu, or any other. The experience at the Mt. Kailash is of pure spiritual awareness of divinity.

The trek to the Kailash Mansorovar is a tough test of endurance and determination. But everyone doing the trek experienced some extra energy that pushed them on, and no one experienced any kind of tiredness after they reached their destination.

The mind loses all senses of physicality and gets completely immersed in the breathtaking beauty of nature, which any human being would at best describe as heavenly!

The sight of the pyramid shaped peak, as if hand chiseled by a master craftsman, the Mt.Kailash radiates an awesome golden glow that makes one mesmerized, forgetting their physical existence. One tends to feel as if they were a part of the limitless expanse of the universe floating as a tiny speck of consciousness and nothing else.

Is that soul-consciousness? Perhaps it is.

And that could be the reason why thousands of sadhus and saints live in the caves of the Himalayas – to experience a close proximity to their God, and to be soul-conscious at all times. Manu too had lived in one such cave for nearly ten years as a pupil of a 120-year-old Himalayan Yogi at a place known as the Gyanganj.

Ved and Malti were stunned to hear Manu's story as to how Manu was nursed back to life after he fell into a gorge and lay almost dead for seven days covered in snow, and how out of nowhere came this Himalayan Yogi, rescued him and took him to his cave and nursed him back to life.

It is hard to believe, but such incidences are quite common in this region and only a few lucky ones with strong past Karma survive to pursue their spiritual journey.

Manu stayed with the Yogi for nearly a decade, before the Yogi sent him to Gupt Kashi, saying that he had some important task to perform.

And it was then that Manu saw in his vision the memories of his past life and knew immediately that Ved and Malti's marriage reunion was to be performed at the divine site of Triyugi Narayan near Gupt Kashi.

And thus, the pre-destined turn of events united the three friends of their past life in this life as well.

Manu was eager to take Ved and Malti to his master – the Himalayan Yogi at the cave near the Kailash Mansorovar.

But the events that followed were something that none of them were prepared for. As they approached the cave, they saw from a distance a bright glow of golden light all around the area where the cave was located. They also saw several tiny glowing dots of light floating around the cave. It was a mesmerizing paranormal sight unfolding in front of their eyes.

They ran the remaining distance and entered the cave amidst an unfamiliar aroma and hazy layers of multi-colored light. And finally, they found the Yogi sitting in a state of transcendental-Samadhi.

Ved and Malti were too dumbfounded to react, but Manu understood. He knew that his master was about to exit from his physical body to merge with his astral body, and attain Nirvana.

Manu signaled to Ved and Malti, and then himself lay prostrate at his master's feet touching his feet.

This was another surreal experience for them, like how Ved had felt in the presence of the Mountain Man when he was transported to a different plane of existence.

They felt a feeling of freshness in their whole body as if being anointed by a soothing balm, and a sensation of cool freshness lifted their spirits to some unknown space of blissfulness.

They were mentally swimming in a state of semi-consciousness when all of a sudden, they were shaken out of their reverie by a burst of energy which lasted barely for a few seconds.

They opened their eyes as an even bigger astonishment unfolded in front of them - something beyond any human experience, and something that only a counted few may have experienced in their lives.

They were jolted awake by a burst of energy. When they opened their eyes, they realized that the Yogi was shedding his physical body. They watched in awe as the five Pranas left the body one at time, one by one, in the form of a brilliant glow of light.Then after having released all the five forms of Prana (life force energies), his soul was departing from the material world.

They were wonder-struck witnessing the most amazing sight of a self-realized soul shedding the physical body after having achieved Nirvana.

This is also referred to as 'Nirvikalpa Samadhi' (attainment of Moksha) in spiritual parlance.

Then in a few blurred moments of vision they witnessed another awesome spectacle – that of the Yogi's soul merging into the Mt. Kailash!

They could see a bright dazzling ball of golden light gradually floating away towards Mt.Kailash, and then in a matter of few seconds expanded into millions of micro pixels, to become one with the mountain.

And at that precise moment, a booming voice greeted them, breaking the magical spell of what they were witnessing.

It was the Mountain Man!

"Welcome to the world of the Himalayan abode, my dear friends," greeted the Mountain Man.

All three of them bowed and expressed their happiness seeing the Mountain Man – their only Cosmo-physical connection to spiritualism in their journey of life.

They cleared some space and placed a floor mat for the Mountain Man to sit, and the three of them sat around him.

"You will gradually get familiar with some of the finer dimensions of a higher plane around here," the Mountain Man said.

Now that you have earned your elevation by the grace of Lord Shiva, and Mahavatar Babaji, you will start a new journey from now on which will take you up the ladder of expanded consciousness.

And once you achieve the desired level of consciousness, you will become eligible to participate in the 'Maha Yajna' at the next Kumbh Mela alongside the Devtas (angels), and Maharshis (saints) who will come to attend the divine Yajna (Vedic ritual).

They listened intently to the Mountain Man and expressed their gratitude for letting them know about their future course of the journey.

The Mountain Man then left, after blessing them by placing the palm of his hand on their head one by one, and at the same time initiating them into the Himalayan tradition of Spiritualism as propagated by Mahavatar Babaji.

Later Manu explained to Ved and Malti that now they have been welcomed into what is commonly described as the 5th dimension of the realm in the soul's journey - a dimension considered to be a higher plane of dwelling for the souls.

Samadhi :

Samadhi is a Sanskrit word mostly used in spiritualism to describe a Yogic state when the practitioner in a deep meditative state blends his body and mind consciousness into his soul consciousness to attain a blissful state of universal consciousness.

'Sama' means 'to be absorbed', 'Dhi' means being in a state of 'Sama'.

It is state of pure and absolute consciousness without any influence by the mind, and awareness of the body. As per the principles of the eight limbs of 'Ashtanga Yoga' all the first seven steps are like the steps of the ladder that leads to the final stage – that of Samadhi.

Though in a common verbal sense Samadhi is also preferred word whenever a saintly person releases his 'Prana' to access death by his own free will, Samadhi is a far larger word associated with 'Nirvana' - the freedom from the cycle of birth.

Samadhi is the highest state of Yogic consciousness and spiritual realization where the awareness of the self, the mind, and the topic of focus of the meditating person merge into oneness, resulting in an 'absolute' state of consciousness.

Samadhi can be generalized in three different forms –

i. The early stage when one's consciousness is in a trance-like state - like in a deep sleep during a hypnotic session - oblivious and yet conscious. This phase is referred to as Laja Samadhi.

ii. The next stage is when in a higher level of consciousness, one gains full control of his thoughts and releases the self completely to remain immersed in his state of blissful consciousness. This phase is called the Savikalpa Samadhi

iii. The third stage is known as Nirvikalpa Samadhi, when one's consciousness is completely absorbed, and is in oneness with the absolute – the supreme consciousness.

Patanjali Yoga-sutras further categorizes Nirvikalpa Samadhi into two broader states – 'Samprajnata Samadhi', and 'Asamprajnata samadhi'.

Samprajnata Samadhi is with a higher knowledge which occurs through the absorption of the mind into an object of concentration; and Asamprajnata is one which is 'beyond higher knowledge', and is a very high state of consciousness in which there is no object of concentration. The only realization here is thus the only of pure and absolute consciousness. In Buddhism, which is another limb of Hinduism, Samadhi is described in four stages of 'Jhana' – which also means meditation.

They are the 1st Jhana, the 2nd Jhana, the 3rd Jhana, and the 4th Jhana.

They eventually correspond to the same state of consciousness as stated in the Patanjali Yoga sutras.

Ved and Malti were too puzzled to understand as to what was going on, as things transpired at such a rapid pace.

Thus, Samadhi can be described as a Yogic meditation where a highest level of consciousness is achieved. It is also a powerful state when enlightenment is achieved and the person is able to shed his body or the mind at will.

Exiting, or shedding the body 'by will', is possible only for those sadhus or monks who possess an extremely higher level of 'absolute consciousness'.

"Breath control is Mind control, Mind control is Self control, and Conquering the Self is conquering Death" Samadhi is also a state when the consciousness of bodily functions of breathing and mental activity ceases to a level of non-existence.

Thus, Samadhi is a state akin to the state of deathlessness.

The term Maha Samadhi is often spoken about when a saintly Yogi transcends from the physical world to the astral world, which we commonly understand as something beyond life and death.

Some sit in meditation and then just release their Prana to attain death, while the others may just vanish into thin air during their meditation.

Swami Hariharananda, a protégé and lineage of Mahavatar Babaji quotes –

'Breath Control is Mind Control, Mind control is Self control, and Self control is death control'

The Maha Samadhi witnessed by Ved, Malti, and Manu was how the Himalayan Yogi sat in a state of Samadhi to shed his body to release his soul consciousness in the form of a bright flame of light into the sky to drift to merge with Lord Shiva at the Kailash Parvat.

This was an enlightening experience for Ved, Malti, and Manu.

***

Chapter VI

Initiation into the Plane of Angels at Kailash Parvat

After the month-long rituals that followed the Maha-Samadhi of the Yogi, several Himalayan sadhus (monks) visited Manu, Ved, and Malti over the next one-and-a-half-year period to pay their respects.

These sadhus were initiated into several schools of spiritual doctrine, and each one of them was an enlightened one.

The Himalayan region was like a Gurukul (ancient boarding schools in an Ashram under a great Guru) for them.

Their training was tough – way beyond any expression of the word tough.

There was no limit to define their mental endurance as well as physical endurance, and the line between their physical endurance limit and mental endurance was a blurred one.

Their day started at 4 am and lasted till late after sunset. No matter which pathway they chose, their ultimate goal was the same – achieving freedom from a finite self to explore the limitless infinite consciousness of the universe after having mastered the physical self of the body and mind, to become a part of time and space.

It was a once in a lifetime opportunity for Ved, Malti, and Manu to meet so many self-realized masters and be blessed by them for the upcoming Maha Kumbh Mela – the biggest spiritual fair on Earth!

Their entire focus now was to become fully prepared for participating in the next upcoming Kumbh Mela at the Triveni (confluence of the three rivers – the Ganga, Yamuna, and Saraswati) at Prayagraj (Allahabad), a city in Uttar Pradesh, India.

And for that, they had to acquire the subtle qualities of elevated consciousness like the Devtas (angels), and also disable the attributes of their 'individual physical self' to become like the Mountain Man – an expanded entity.

This necessitated not only extreme elevated abilities of abstinence and penance, but also become receivers of abundance of divine grace.

Several Himalayan yogis guided them in their endeavor because they were well aware of the fact that the three of them were to play an important role in representing the 'cause' during the Maha-Yajna (Vedic ritual) that was to be performed at the 144th Maha Kumbh Mela.

Being 'Twin Flames' by precedence, they were elevated souls and were superior beings compared to ordinary humans. Ved and Malti were also endowed with initiation into Kriya Hatha Yoga by Mahavatar Babaji himself. Hence, they were chosen to participate at the mega Mela.

Manu too, fitted in as he had acquired a high level of Karmic achievement. He had meditated at the foot of the Mount Kailash for prolonged periods and was also sensitive to the subtle energies of the universe.

They undertook a rigorous 16-18 hours a day of the toughest schedule every day and at times remained isolated from any human association for months together without any food and water, and thereby transcending their consciousness of their physical self to float in the vast expanse of limitless universal consciousness, and experiencing the bliss and harmony of the 'Sat-Chitta-Anandam' (a state of pure, and permanent bliss).

Their daily bath at the Mansorovar in the wee hours of the Brahm-muhurt (auspicious period of time in the early morning at 4 am) charged them with enough divine energy to go through the day that was filled with arduous tasks which otherwise would have not been possible. The bath and the rinse in the holy waters of the Mansarovar cleansed them of any impurity of the body, mind, and the soul.

After eighteen months of self-induced isolation and abstinence from everything physical, they acquired a psychic awareness of soul-consciousness that was beyond the realm of dwellers of the physical world on the planet earth.

One specific event that stood out during their training period as a part of the training was when the Mountain Man initiated them into the Tantric wisdom of the 'Sri Yantra'.

Ved, Malti and Manu were made to sit in the formation of an equilateral triangle, and the Mountain Man sat at the central point of the triangle. This was a Kriya (ritual) taken directly out of the SRI YANTRA that would enable the three of them to acquire some critical universal energies in great detail.

The three of them were guided by the Mountain Man to sit in meditative posture and then align (centering) their focus on to his third eye of the Mountain Man.

It was an impossible task for all three of them to look at the third eye of the Mountain Man at the same time but when they closed their eyes to meditate, each of them was able to look at the third eye of the Mountain Man, all at the same time.

For any onlooker, it would appear that the Mountain Man was sitting at the center of the triangle, but his face had a 360-degree visibility emanating from the central point, which was free of any specific dimension - length, breath, and depth.

As their concentration grew in intensity, several layers of lights in the form of a powerful beam began to form, connecting the three of them with the Mountain Man, and trisecting the original one single triangle into three different triangles.

And these beams of light began to multiply forming several multiple new triangles of light, accompanied by a humming sound – the sound of the cosmos - AUM.It was a sight to behold - one that was psychedelic in nature and that expanded consciousness.

They remained in that state for seven consecutive days.

Seven days sitting in one position without moving was practically unbelievable, but everything was possible when one transcended the gross level of physical existence to the subtle level of micro cosmic consciousness.

(Ref. Soruba Samadhi – Grace of Mahavatar Babaji's Kriya Yoga)

Their meditation ended on the eighth day when a wave of cold air brushed against their faces and they were jolted awake, only to find that it was awfully quiet there, and the Mountain Man had gone.

They had lost all track of time and had not eaten or slept for the last seven days. Yet they felt surprisingly fresh and full of energy. Their mind was crystal clear, and an unusual feeling of calm.

Then they began to remember slowly what they have been doing for the last seven days. They were surprised to become aware with total clarity that now they had digested the entire wisdom contained inside the SRI YANTRA and about the universal play of energies, and the basic sciences of Sansarik Manifestation - the fundamentals upon which the operation and management of the universe happened, including those of our planet earth, and a host of other facts that a normal human being with their limited amount of consciousness could never comprehend.

They felt as if now they belonged at another plane of existence.

It was fascinating for them to realize that how so much had changed in them in such a short period of time, having transcended from ordinary human beings to such an expanded level of wisdom and consciousness.

They crossed past the barrier of gross and became a part of the subtle by acquiring a level of consciousness that parleyed with a non-linear state of all pervading universal being.

Now they had mastered the concepts of the five elements that supported the creation of life on our planet.

They also mastered the sciences of the Chakras, the Pranas (life force energies), and the five subtle elements of life consciousness – the cellular body (Tan), the mental body (Man), the cellular Prana (life force energies), the intellectual body (Gyan), and finally the celestial awareness of emotional body (Anahata – heart chakra).

No fire could burn them now, and neither would any freezing temperature affect their sensory organs.

Walking on a bed of fire or walking on the surface of water was just a thought to make it happen, and nothing appeared to matter anymore, as their physicality had transcended the shackles of the limited self.

Their awareness of their physical body too was just a thought now, and their Aham (ego) dissolved to a level that didn't matter anymore.

And yet they remained in their human body like before as they had to play an important role at the Kumbh Mela, to sit alongside the Saptarshis, and the other divine celestials who visited our planet during the Kumbh Mela to perform the rituals to revive the flow of 'Amrit' - the elixir of life force energies from the Kamandal for the sustenance of the human-ecosystem.

The protectors of the Himalayan order of the spiritualism prepared for this event for more than three years to get everything right for this rare grace of visiting our planet earth by the angels at the Maha Kumbh Mela, and most importantly to safeguard the Kamandal when it manifested as a result of the Amrit-Manthan (retrieval).

And after a rigorous 18 months of trial by fire, Ved, Manu, and Malti were ready to take their hot seats alongside the Dev-Rishis, and the Saptrishis to perform the Vedic-Yajna rituals.

On one auspicious eleventh day (Ekadasi) of the lunar cycle they set out on their journey on foot from the Kailash Mansarovar to Prayagraj – where the Maha Kumbh Mela was to take place.

And unseen and unknown to them, thousands of other sadhus, Naga-Sadhus, and Akharas too started their journey from thousands of unseen and unknown caves in the Himalayas to the greatest fair (Mela) on Earth – the Kumbh Mela that was to begin in a month's time.

***

Chapter VII
KUMBH MELA (The Kumbh Fair)

The Kumbh Mela is a spiritual fair held every three years at four locations across India – Prayagraj (City of Allahabad), Haridwar, Ujjain, and Nasik.

The Mela returns to each center after a gap of 12 years.

The Kumbh Mela held at Prayagraj at the confluence of the three rivers Ganga, Yamuna, and Saraswati, holds a unique significance because of the merging of the holy waters of the three rivers that have spiritual significance.

The three rivers hold spiritual relevance during the Kumbh Mela with respect to life, and sustenance of Samsara – the human eco system.

The river Ganga descended on Earth at the behest of Lord Shiva to enable humans to cleanse their sins by the waters of Goddess Ganga. Thus, the holy dip during the Mela is meant to cleanse sins from the Samsara.

Yamuna river is a highly revered and worshipped river because she is the daughter of the Sun God, and the sister of the God of Death -Yama. Thus, she holds a position of relevance with regards to 'Prana' – life, and death. She stimulated Life, and relieved the pain of Death.

Saraswati which flowed in the north western part of India some 5000 years ago, seems to have disappeared physically, but remains in metaphysical form and materializes at the confluence, only during the 'Shahi-Snan' – the holy dip during the Kumbh Mela. Goddess Saraswati is believed to enhance life- procreation, and also played an important role in enhancing spirituality in humans. It is important to note that the river Saraswati is a part incarnation of Ma Saraswati – spouse of Lord Brahma.

The Mela (fair) also provided an opportunity for the people to get a taste of divinity and a chance to wash away sins by taking a dip in the charged holy waters of the three rivers.

Worshippers line up early morning at 4 am on the day of 'Mauni Amavashya' – an auspicious day of the moon's astrological configuration, and charge into the water behind the ascetics and sadhus amidst the beating of drums and sounds of conch shell in a frenzy of cacophony.

However, due to the large number of worshippers, they are allowed only a quick dip, lasting no more the 30-40 seconds.

The Kumbh Mela held at the other three centers are called 'Ardh Kumbh', or Half-Kumbh Mela and are held on the banks of only one river – Ganges in Haridwar; Godavari in Nasik; and Shipra in Ujjain.

A vast mega pop-up 'tent city' is built around the Prayagraj basin for the visitors to the Mela.

According to BBC reports, the budget for the oncoming Mela is about four-five hundred million Indian rupees, and the budget goes up every time.

Civic amenities such as emergency medical tents, about 100,000 drinking water depots, emergency medical first aid centers with doctors and nurses, ambulance services, about 150,000 odd toilets, several makeshift auditoriums, provisions for spiritual ritual sites for the several Akharas of the sadhus and monks, etc are some of the basic infrastructure for the mega pop-up city constructed for the Mela.

Advanced electronic monitoring systems are deployed towards smooth management during the fair, to tackle stampede, disasters, and the 'lost and found' issues, which are very common occurrences during such a mega mela of humanity.

The unseen presence of divinity during the Kumbh Mela and the pointers to their effect on the visitors to the Mela provided a unique sense of mysticism and expectation of miracles during the Mela.

Yet, not all visitors to the Mela are aware about the subtle intrinsic connection that this Mela has vis-à-vis the management of the affairs of the universe during the present Yug (Kali Yug), and that of the planet Earth.

It is a rare opportunity for the seekers of the truth to experience some heavenly activity if they were lucky.

Thus, for some it was just a visit to a religious fair, while for those who were involved at a much higher level of perception, this Mela held a profound significance.

The 'Sapta-Rishis' (the Seven Sages – the bearer of divine wisdom) who correspond to the 'seven-star' of the big dipper of the Ursa Major constellation, the 'Prajapati'- the designated ruler of the universe, Lord Shiva – the one who is all pervading, and who sat at the peak of the Mt.Kailash at the center of the celestial eco-sphere, Lord Vishnu, Lord Brahma (the TRINITY of Hinduism) are all believed to descend at the site of this fair to re-infuse the elixir of Prana-Amrit, the seeds of life on our planet.

The KUMBH MELA is a baffling event with layers and layers of mysterious game of cosmic events that are played out at a gross level on planet Earth, where Gods mingled with the humans.

The congregation of millions of sadhus (monks), saints, scholars and philosophers of the Hindu faith, and also seekers of truth from across the globe, is held only at a specific date according to the configuration of the astrological chart, and held at four astrologically strategic locations in India.

The anecdote behind the Kumbh Mela refer to a curse that was given by the 'angry-Rishi' Durvasa to Lord Indra, the king of the Devtas (angels) for insulting and torturing a Rishi, while he was in deep meditation. The curse was that Indra and all the other Devtas (angels) would lose their 'Sri' (angelic sheen), divinity and their powers.

The curse resulted in a chaos that unsettled the management of God's creation to survive, and darkness engulfed the universe.

In a frantic effort to save the universe from the curse of the angry Rishi Durvasa, the Devtas approached Lord Shiva for a way out.

Lord Shiva summoned Rishi Durvasa for a solution to this problem that arose because of his curse, and Rishi Durvasa advised that a ritual of *'Samudra Manthan' be carried out from the Kumbh (ovum) of the ocean. From the Samudra-Manthan would immerge many valuable gifts, and one of them would be a 'Kamandal'.

The 'Kamndal' is a pitcher (pot) containing Amrit – the elixir of life, which will then re-infuse Prana (life force energies) in the universe, and which will then neutralize the curse. Thus the 'Samudra Manthan' would revive the life and bring the creation back to normal.

> **Samudra Manthan:** 'Samudra' means the Ocean, and 'Manthan' means to churn. The churning of the waters of the ocean initially resulted in throwing up of the sins and toxins of humanity (poisonous substances), and later threw up gifts that accumulated from the good karma and the efforts of the Rishis, Sadhus and Saints. The ultimate gift from the Samudra Manthan was the 'Kamandal' containing the 'Amrit' – the Elixir of Life.

Lord Shiva then advised the Devtas (angels) to perform the Samudra Manthan with the help of the Asuras (power seeking demons of lower wisdom), and to churn the ocean to extract the Kamandal containing the elixir of life – the Amrit.

As it turned out, it was a job easier said than done.

The Asuras hated the Devtas and didn't trust them. They were always on the opposite end of the pole. The Devtas found themselves in a catch 22 situation.

They had no option, but to once again beg Lord Shiva to find a solution.

Lord Shiva then took it upon himself to convince the Asuras to participate in the 'Samudra-Manthan' to retrieve the Kamandal for the greater good for everyone. He also assured the Asuras that that they too would be given an equal opportunity to share the 'Amrita' which would give them a chance to become equal to the Devtas (angels).

Thus, the ritual for retrieval of the Kamandal from the ovum of the ocean was initiated by the trinity of Gods Lord Shiva, Lord Vishnu, and Lord Brahma.

The effort to churn out Amrita (Elixir of Life) was a unique concerted effort, together by the 'privileged' Devtas and the 'under privileged' Asuras, at the behest of Lord Shiva to provide an equal opportunity to both – the Devtas and the Asuras, signifying that God held an unbiased attitude for both - putting them on either sides of a 'weighing balance' of the justice system.

It also reflected that the co-habitation of the both 'good' and 'evil' was important, just like the light and the darkness, day and night, and 'Sukha' and 'Dukha' (Joy and Sorrow) - to keep the concept of Life alive.

The churning threw up the poisons first (sins of the humanity), and because of this, the entire planet was about to be poisoned to extinction.

Lord Shiva came to the rescue by drinking all the poison that came out, thus saving the planet from being poisoned. Since then, Lord Shiva came to be known as 'Neel Kantha' – one with a blue throat as his throat became blue when he drank the Halahal (the poison). Followed by the churning out of the poison, several precious and valuable gifts were churned out from the ovary of the ocean.

One such precious divine gift was a symbolic 'Mother Cow'. This Cow was known as 'Kamdhenu' – one who could provide anything that one asked for.

Later, when the Amrit Kamandal was churned out, a tussle erupted between the Devtas and the Asuras (the angels and the demons) to grab the Amrita.

Conceptually this tussle signifies the tussle between the good and the evil in our human eco system.

The Kumbh Mela that is performed in our present Kali Yug is a continuation of the above concept of Samudra Manthan, and is held after every 144 years, albeit in a slightly different manner compared to the Samudra Manthan.

The tradition of this event of retrieving the Kamandal from the Kumbh (the ovary/ the pit) was re-started at the confluence of the three rivers (Triveni Sangam) at Rudra Prayag, in the city of Allahabad in India.

The significance of the Maha Kumbh Mela is described in detail in the Hindu scriptures of the Vishnu Puran, Bhagwat Puran, and the Mahabharata (an epic of the Hindu religion).

The event is being held since the beginning of human civilization towards invoking Lord Shiva, and Lord Vishnu's grace for the survival and wellbeing of the universe – and to detoxify the planet of all the toxic elements for the eco-system to survive, aka, the cleansing, detoxifying and rejuvenating our planet earth for a 144 yearly maintenance program.

The basic difference between the original Samudra Manthan and the present one is that, in the original one a mountain was used to churn the water of the ocean with the help a huge snake (Vasuki) wrapped around the mountain and pulled from two sides to rotate the mountain, the head side of the snake being held by the Devtas (angels), and the tail side of the snake by the Asuras (demons).

In the present day Kumbh Mela, the churning happens naturally when the rushing waters of the three rivers converge at one point creating a cyclonic effect on the water like a twister cyclone, thereby throwing up everything upward from the eye of the storm towards the sky.

How so ever hypothetical this may sound, the philosophical thought behind it applies to a cleansing process of the human eco-System and at the psychological level, is a periodic cleansing of sins of the human race.

The participation of the divinity during the Kumbh Mela is quite relevant at our present age when our planet is in a precarious situation, struggling to survive the ecological destruction and the resultant global warming, air pollution, sea water levels rising due to melting of the glaciers and so on.

And without the intervention from the divinity, the creation could not survive. The word 'Kamandal' is referred to Lord Shiva's pitcher that he always carried in his hands, just also as the Rishis did, with Ganga jal (waters from the Ganges) in it, to sprinkle to purify sins where ever they went.

Lord Shiva is always seen carrying a 'Trishul' (trident) with a 'Damru' (a small two-headed handheld drum) attached to the trident, and a Kamandal in his other hand.

There have been several lineages of belief systems followed by different sections of the society regarding the interpretation of divinity in the Kumbh Mela.

It is believed that the 'Sapta Rishis' appeared in human form to participate in the 'Yajna' ('Havan', a Vedic fire ritual amidst the chanting of Mantras), to awaken the grace of Lord Shiva for raising the Kamandal.

The sacred rituals are very powerful mediums for invoking the powers of the divinity, and conducted by groups of realized sages and sadhus (monks). The rituals performed at the Mela are at an elevated plane of consciousness, and is believed to be an interactive invocation ceremony performed by the humans and the divinity together, that made the Kumbh extraction possible – just as how the Samudra Manthan was done by both – the angels and the Asuras.

The Kumbh Mela is hosted by thousands of sadhus and fakirs who otherwise were never to be seen amidst the society, and who spend their lives hidden in the Himalayan caves doing their 'Tapa' – a form of meditative abstinence under complete isolation and being in a state of transcendence for months together.

They happened to be the guardians of the Himalayan tradition of spiritualism – those who harmonized with the Himalayas and the vibrations of the Kailash Parvat, and couldn't be traced or identified individually.

They come to the Kumbh Mela to get the grace of the 'Sapt Rishis' and also to participate in the 'Yajna', and most importantly, to experience the celestial aura at the Kumbh Mela.

When these sadhus come out to attend the Kumbh Mela, they draw huge crowds.

People from all walks of life come out to see these sadhus who abandoned family life in their pursuit of God, and also out of curiosity to see their lifestyle and behavior, or to get spiritual tips from them and their blessings.

The naked 'Naga Sadhus' and the 'Aghoris' are a major attraction during the Kumbh Mela because of their unorthodox attire and unpredictable behavior, with total disregard for any sort of social norms of behavior and conduct. They are also known to be devotees of Shiva, and the use of drugs like 'Aafim', and 'Ganja' (raw form of Marijuana / Cannabis) are an inherent part of their 'Huka-Chillum' lifestyle.

SOME HIGHLIGHTS OF THE KUMBH MELA:

As mentioned earlier - the churning of the ocean (Sagar Manthan) produced several valuable gifts for humanity and its welfare, the Kumbh Mela too gave humanity a go, once again to revive life on this planet.

Some of those that became a part and parcel of the take-away from the Kumbh Mela are described below –

THE SHAHI SNAN:

The Shahi Snan is primarily one of the most important objective of the Maha Kumbh Mela when millions of the masses get an opportunity to take a holy dip in the waters at the 'Triveni-Sangam', to rinse all their sins amidst the presence of divinity, and amidst the highly charged spiritualistic ambiance and the most auspicious astrological configuration of the 'Grahas' (the stars) on the day of 'Mauni Amavashya'.

The faith, and trust on this ritual has a much deeper religious connotation than most people not familiar with Hinduism could comprehend.

The Sun, as per Hindu philosophy plays a very important supportive role in the creation and sustenance of life-form on our planet, and hence is worshipped in numerous ways in Hindu philosophy.

And the holy dip in conjunction with a 'Sun salutation' is a stipulated ritual because the purpose of the Maha Kumbh Mela too is to rinse the sins of the humanity, and towards re-infusing 'Prana' in our planet.

Some of the most practiced ways of Sun worship are – 'the Surya Pranam' (salutation to the Sun) – a twelve step yogic procedure. 'Surya Yoga' is an interactive meditation with the Sun as the center of focus, and 'the Surya Jal offering' is a practice of offering water and prayers to the Sun, are a few that are commonly practiced by followers in Hindu religion towards a prolific affluence of procreative activity in our planet.

TANTRISM:

It is a secret from the Himalayan tradition of spiritualism, and an attraction at the Kumbh Mela, lures a big number of seekers.

Tantrism is Lord Shiva's gift to humanity and is a science that is practiced by exponents of the art in a ritualistic procedure to invoke energies of the universe for the wellbeing and preservation of the universe in an effective manner.

Such are the powers of Tantrism that unbelievable miracles could be performed by its practitioners.

These practitioners lived a very 'un-worldly' kind of life that enabled them to be channels of universal energies.

Needless to say, a number of unscrupulous Tantriks used Tantrism for their nefarious objectives.

A number of fraudsters too come to enjoy the free-flowing supply of drugs and intoxicants in the name of practicing Tantrism during the Kumbh Mela. These fraud Tantriks also become easy targets of the power hungry politicians, and criminals as well.

Sri Yantra:

'SRI-YANTRA' is an astral app, if I may call it that, attracts thousands of Astro-physicists to the Kumbh Mela, as it is believed that quite a few spiritual masters and gurus descend at the site of the Kumbh Mela to spread the wisdom of the Sri Yantra to the seekers.

Sri-Yantra is a powerful tool that represents the un-manifested powers and facets of the Universe.

The 'Yantra' (tool/design) consists of nine constituent triangles that intersect each other to form forty-three smaller triangles, organized at five concentric levels.

In the middle of the Sri-Yantra lies the 'Bindu' (a dot/or fulcrum) representing the source of origin of everything in the universe, as well as of all realms beyond.

SRI-YANTRA is the geometric representation of the entire Cosmos, and in it resides everything – the good, the evil, and other astrological configurations influencing the 'life form' on our planet.

Anyone with adequate wisdom of the Sri Yantra could use it for calculating the algorithm of the geo-astrological predictions.

But a unique SRI –YANTRA - the tool used by the self-realized Rishis, like the Himalayan masters, is a prized Yantra (tool) that no ordinary human could handle except for one single time i.e during the Kumbh Mela held after every 144 years.

THE KAMANDAL:

It is believed that at the start of 'life-form' on our planet, a divine 'Kamandal' (a brass pitcher) that contained the elixir of life sprinkled the essence of Life into our planet.

Till such time this elixir from the Kamandal is replenished, a Yug (a celestial period of existence) lasted, and at the end of a Yug the Kamandal hibernated till a next Yug was started after being activated again by divine providence.

The periodic Yug-system (span of existence of life form) - four of them in Hindu philosophy, is a specific period of existence of life form - each Yug lasting five thousand solar years or so (the configuration of the figure may be a variable for each Yug).

After the completion of three such Yugs, the present one - 'Kali Yug' is in progress, and as it appears, this Yug too is fast nearing its end.

A number of tell-tale signs are becoming all too visible – the infrequent floods and Tsunamis, the unpredictable weather-related disasters, the forest fires, the random killings and acts of terrorism, the wars, and a general wave of intolerance and aggression amongst humanity in general, clearly signals that Kali Yug is nearing its end now.

With the oncoming Maha Kumbh Mela after 144 years, and in anticipation of retrieval of the Kamandal during this Kumbh Mela, numerous forces of evil will become active to try and lay their hands on the Kamandal.

Though the possession of the Kamandal remained unconquered in any of the previous Yugs so far, a tug of war between the good and the evil happens each and every time the Kamandal is raised.

The SRI VIDYA Path of Spiritualism:

It's been documented that the 'Sri Vidya' is an integral part of the Himalayan tradition of spiritualism and is a method of Tantric worship with the aim to obtain definite objectives as desired by the practitioners. 'Sri' means wellness and self-development, and 'Vidya' means wisdom for 'Sri' to materialize.

Concepts of Sri Vidya propagate the principles that an individual self and the universal principles are intertwined. One cannot be understood without studying the other. Only by studying and analyzing the self can one understand the principles of the universe.

Sri Vidya analyzed the potential of the universe, and hence that of God, by interpreting God's 'Will', 'Knowledge', and God's 'Expression' of His 'Will', and 'Knowledge' with respect to His creation.

Sri Vidya is studied to understand the science of energy fields that link our gross physical world with the subtle metaphysical world.

Sri Vidya arose from the great Shakti tradition of Tantrism with the primary objective of total focus on SHAKTI (the 'Purush-Prakriti' concept in Hindu philosophy.

Numerous 'Tatvas' (postulates- theories about wisdom) were made available to the wise men by the study of the Sri Yantra, to be shared with the people and also to spread them far and wide across the globe for strengthening the protocols of the social moral code of behavior, and also as a means of guidance to live a truthful and righteous life of 'Dharma' for one's Karma (actions) in a righteous way.

These Tatvas (postulates), established the roots of a new world order of spiritualism towards stabilizing humanity, and the epicenter of the source of management of the creation being at the Mt. Kailash where Lord Shiva sat (The 'Adi Yogi', the eternal entity).

Shiva is described as 'One who is', and yet 'One who isn't', meaning one who is there all pervading, yet one who cannot be identified. Humans too, created in the same image of Shiva, live for a brief period life under an assumed identity and then perishes, but his/her real identity – the soul, remains alive, and unperishable.

Later the 18 Siddhas – the direct descent of Lord Shiva's initiates travelled far and wide across the globe to spread the wisdom of Lord Shiva's Tatvas, as has been documented and the relics of which are still found in countries such as Indonesia, Cambodia, Vietnam, Japan, Malaysia and the Mayan civilization of South America to name a few.

***

Chapter VIII
THE CONSPIRACY

The celestial moment (Mahurat) for this Maha Kumbh Mela after a gap of 144 years, has a great significance in terms of the ecological management and the sustenance of the geo-physical aspects with respect to life on this planet.

The Mountain Man and Mahavatar Babaji had given sufficient hints to Ved, Malti, and Manu that the present Maha Kumbh Mela would not only be a very special one, but also one with some very serious hurdles.

There were plenty of indications that some significant disturbances were anticipated during this Maha Kumbh Mela - to sabotage the actual Vedic ritual of raising the Kamandal containing the 'Amrit', by a group of sorcerers from China with the help of the legendary evil spirit of Yaku Xi.

The Story of Yaku Xi:

The saga of Yaku Xi, a fugitive Buddhist monk goes way back to the 11th century, when Saint Milerappa, and Sorcerer

Naro Bonchung faced each other in a fierce battle to gain power in the Tibetan belt of Kailash Parvat - a tussle between the good and the evil, and Yaku Xi's tale is an extension of the same.

Yaku Xi, initially a disciple of Milereppa, was lured away by Naro Bonchung, who trained him, and who later become a legendary Satan and sorcerer.

When we look at history, we will find that every Yug produced an evil Satan capable of challenging God, and Yaku Xi was one such evil soul with unparalleled powers.

A master 'shape-shifter', Yaku Xi's life panned out across many a century, first in flesh and blood in the 11th century, and then in numerous shapes of an evil spirit till the 21st century.

Yaku Xi tormented the protectors of the spiritualism of the Himalayan tradition for hundreds of years till Devin, a prodigy of Mahavatar Babaji, and later as Ramunna, an incarnation of Devin in his next birth, put an end to the saga of Yaku Xi - the evil spirit.

Or so it was believed.

The general belief was that the evil spirit of Yaku Xi was vanquished during the 1962 Chinese aggression of India when the Chinese army had to make a sudden retreat and flee in the face of some astonishing celestial warfare never seen by humanity before.

It is still a popular topic of bon-fire discussions in the cold Bhutanese town of Bomdila, about how Yaku Xi's spirit had a direct role to play during the People's Liberation Army of China's aggression on India in their endeavor to grab control over the entire region panning from the Kailash Mansarovar up to the Tawang region of the Arunachal Pradesh in India.

It sounds a bit too profound for a modern mind to digest such superstitious beliefs but in the context of the broader spectrum of the actual events, no one can deny the supernatural activity that people saw with their own eyes on that fateful morning on the hills of Bomdila that led to the fleeing of the Chinese Army helter-skelter in a state of panic. Devin, a disciple of Mahavatar Babaji, was a master in the art of performing the sacred rituals of 'Hiranya-Garbha' and many other secret wisdom of the 'Sri Vidya' procedures of 'Tantrism', such as - reading the algorithm of the sacred 'Sri Yantra' to awaken the vibrations of many secret and dormant energies of the universe, art of 'thunder and lightning warfare', and the last but not the least, the most holiest act of manifesting the 'Kamandal' from the Hiranya-Garbha.

The enigma of the Chinese invasion of India (Taichung, as the Chinese called India in those days) when the PLA of China invaded India via the Bhutanese territory of Bomdila in 1962, is still not known to the people from other parts of the world even now.

Even though the two nations had just signed an agreement of 'Panchsheel'- a five principle peace treaty in 1953 with a famous slogan *"Hindi-Chini Bhai Bhai"* (India-China brotherhood), it was at the behest of the occultist gang of perpetrators of Yaku Xi who convinced the PLA commanders to invade India.

(That was a primitive China those days in the early sixties, underdeveloped and cut off from rest of the world economy).

That the entire 1962 operation was shrouded in mystery and very few, including the Government of India had any clue as to what happened and why it happened.

But there is an interesting tale attached to this mystery that brought the Chinese invasion to an abrupt end.

The folklore has it that Devin and his five friends (popularly known as the DWARF) unleashed several forms of Cosmic-warfare on Yaku Xi's spirit, and the accompanying Chinese Army.

The story of the DWARF is narrated in the soon to be published 3rd part of the trilogy of this book, titled 'Kamandal'.

The sight of the terrifying sounds of thunder, and showers of lightning raining on the Chinese Army on a clear early dawn sky and the accompanying heat generated that burnt everything on ground to ashes.

The occultist army of Yaku Xi, and Yaku Xi himself perished during this psychedelic warfare, and that resulted in sudden retreat by the remaining Chinese Army from the war.

This story of Yaku Xi's demolition stood ground for almost half a century, till now when new evidence surfaced that the spirit of Yaku Xi was resurrected once again by twelve Chinese occultists.

The Present Conspiracy:

The news of an unusual activity of occultist ritual by a group of twelve Chinese priests came to the notice of the sadhus residing in Himalayan plateau.

Gradually their occult-rituals gained momentum, and such was the intensity generated by their powers that a majority of the sadhus residing in the hidden caves of the Himalayas had to flee for safety, and converged at the Kailash Mansarovar lake seeking protection from Lord Shiva.

The Chinese attempts to take over the spiritual control of the Mt. Kailash region has been an unfulfilled quest since thousands of years. After having taken control of Tibet now they are trying in different ways to achieve their goal.

The Maha Kumbh Mela is presently their target towards achieving the same objective.

The Chinese occultists who had managed to steal a part of the secret scripts of the Vedic rituals at the Hiranya-Garbha from some Buddhist monks from the famous monastery at Tawang, now wanted to make an all-out attempt to steal the rest of the scriptures and the know-how, to gain control of the management of Life on our planet.

And towards this objective, the 12 evil Chinese perpetrators were able to invoke the spirit of the dreaded Yaku Xi using the very same secret mantras that they had used to steal earlier from the Buddhist monastery at Tawang.

This was a disturbing moment of truth that the very same powerful wisdom of the Tantrik sciences that Lord Shiva had gifted to mankind for their welfare, was now being used to destroy mankind.

And once again, the responsibility of saving the universal eco-system, and thereby the mankind fell upon the able grace of Mahavatar Babaji.

And to that objective Babaji put forth an active team to tackle any obstruction that may arise during the Kumbh Mela.

Babaji initiated Ved, Malti, and Manu as the main players, backed by large group of Himalayan sadhus to safeguard the Hiranya-Garbha arena where the raising of the Kamandal ceremony was to be performed.

The presence of Babaji himself, the Mountain Man and many other Daivik entities would be present over the arena - unseen to the human eye.

Priyadarshini Raghuvanshi, aka Priya:

A vivacious and dynamic journalist Priyadarshini was invited by Ved to attend the Kumbh Mela to keep a watch over the daily proceedings, and to cover her experiences for a journal to be published later.

She readily agreed and was overjoyed at the opportunity.

Earlier Priya had covered the Bhimtal earthquake incident as a freelancer for BBC and had later interviewed Ved and Malti in an extensive interview over a period of 2-3 days. Her interview had opened up a whole new perception of life for her, and it surprised her that how a majority of us lived a life of so much ignorance. Her mind now began to open up to a much broader view of life, and quite a few new doors opened up for her to explore life. Her mind filled up with gratitude for Ved and Malti for clearing many layers of cobweb of ignorance that had blurred her vision of life.

Since then on, Priya had followed Ved and Malti's life as best as she could to quench her curiosity about the higher truths of life.

On learning from Yukta and Yamini about Ved and Malti's 'twin-flame' indoctrination at Triyugi Narayan at Guptkashi, she had once again attended the celestial marriage ceremony. And what she had witnessed there confirmed her faith in spirituality manifold, and mostly accepted Ved and Malti as 'Mahan-Atma' (superior souls).

Now she felt privileged that Ved had invited her to attend the Kumbh Mela.Priya, also as a confidential informer for the RAW, the intelligence wing of the Indian Defense Services, was given the task of pursuing any Chinese involvement, and activity during the Mela, on the basis of inputs from chatter intercepted by the RAW.

Thus, it was not just a coincidence that Priya became a part of a big Chinese conspiracy that was about to unfold at the 144th Kumbh Mela.

Surely Babaji had a role to play in her induction to the team.

Thus, a very skeptical investigative journalist Priya landed at Prayagraj amidst the colorful chaos of the Maha Kumbh Mela and blended with the sea of humanity gathered there.

It was big proud moment for Priya.

She wanted to unearth the truth behind the rumors of the secrets of this periodic 144th edition of Kumbh Mela.

She did a lot of homework collecting information and preparing well in advance about this Mela by visiting remote areas of spiritual sites in the Himalayas, and by interviewing many Naga Sadhus and Aghori Sadhus, and from the information she gathered she learnt about the twelve Chinese perpetrators.

And yet, little did she know that she would herself play a role in unmasking these perpetrators and expose the Chinese conspiracy of a supernatural nature during the Mela.

Armed with her skepticism and determination Priya didn't have much difficulty in infiltrating the inner circle of spiritual leaders associated with the Mela Management Committee.

As she mingled with the Mela crowd, she was overawed by the vast sea of humanity, and at the same time was astonished to see to the extent in which faith, ignorance, superstition merged.

The unseen playground of spirituality that prevailed at one single venue and under one sky was as daunting a task for her as perhaps climbing the Everest, but she was determined to do her best to analyze the ground zero facts as best as she could.

She met Ved and Malti, who in turn introduced her to a number of other the members of the Management Committee including the DCP (Deputy Commissioner of Police) who was in-charge of the security during the Mela.

Manu provided her with the much-needed background and information about Kumbh Mela that she never thought existed, and that were beyond her comprehension.

She was not the type who believed in things that she could not verify, yet she couldn't disregard the information that Manu provided her. She trusted Manu completely.

As she delved deeper into the heart of the congregation, she began to witness numerous inexplicable phenomenon and experiences that challenged her rational beliefs.

Meanwhile, within the secretive Mela Management Committee, the scholars and rishis, tension grew as they navigated ancient prophecies, and also the news of intrusion by the Chinese perpetrators.

They feared for the worst, as the weight of their divine responsibilities kept them on tenterhooks.

The fate of the world rested on their shoulders for the successful completion of the ritual to retrieve the Kamandal to rejuvenate afresh the seeds of Life on our planet.

As Priya's investigation on the Mela continued, the line between her skepticism and the optics of spirituality became blurred.

Little did she know that Mahavatar Babaji was behind her guiding her in her mission.

She was forced to confront her own beliefs and her skepticism while navigating a world of supernatural occurrences amidst the gross physical reality of humanity.

Hence 'The Maha Kumbh Mela' was for her an exploration of faith, skepticism and of spirituality.

The human quest for eternal life turned out to be a mesmerizing tale set against the backdrop of one of the world's most significant spiritual gatherings – the Maha Kumbh Mela.

She was treading on a space where no one in their proper senses would dare, crossing the boundaries of reality and supernatural.

The strange lifestyle of the Aghoris fascinated her – seeing them eating raw half cooked meat, smoking 'bhang' in 'chillums' (a thin earthen smoker's pot), their bodies smudged with ashes from the cremated human bodies from crematoriums, made her wonder as to what faith this form of spirituality garnered!

The story of the Naga Sadhus was yet another intriguing facet of spirituality that she could not quite fathom.

They did not wear any clothes. They lived in the freezing cold Himalayas without any clothes – believe that?

There were many more stuff like that, which Priya made notes of, in her journal.

It was a stunning journey that explored the power of faith, the mysteries of the universe, and the potential for transformation through the convergence of spirituality and science.

What alarmed her most was the extent of superstition amongst the naïve and vulnerable 'Aastikas' (believers) who thronged the Mela in search of miracles. And rightly so, because miracles happen in this great country of India too often!

It was not until one day, when she inadvertently happened to witness an astonishing un-nerving incident.

Late one evening, when she was summing up her daily report in her computer, she became aware of a very foul stench emanating from outside. She ignored it for a while but became curious about it as this was not a usual kind of smell. Mostly such smells were common for the local people, and often went unnoticed. But with her trained and alert mind, she became instantly curious, and decided to investigate. She came outside of her tent to trace the source of the smell but couldn't find anything. The smell was real she thought, so it had to have a source. So, she decided to continue her search.

She walked about half a mile – away from the campus, towards a bushy ridge. The smell was quite intense there and she felt a shiver of fear alerting her of an imminent danger. Then she saw a dried-up drain that disappeared into a deep pit.

There she found a dried up well.

It wasn't deep, may be about five feet or so, and with a circular steps that led into the pit of the well.

When she went down the steps up to the pit, she saw an opening that led into a passage, and some light was emanating from inside. It was a well-hidden cave!

And as she went closer, to the entrance of the cave, she heard some weird sounds coming from inside.

All her instincts warned her not to venture any further, but her professional instinct prodded her on. She lamented the fact that she didn't carry her professional camera as she went in deeper towards the cave.

She realized that she had reached a point of no return and found herself creeping into the cave.

The cave forked out into two large passages, and one led to a room where an occult ritual was in progress. The other passage led to an large opening and it was a fully equipped electronic monitoring room with TV screens, cameras, computers that covered every nook and corner of the Kumbh Mela ground.

She managed to find a convenient spot to hide herself in the computerized monitoring room from where she was able to look into the other room where the occult ceremony was in progress.

The site of a live black magic ritual in progress was nauseating and she felt like puking. The smell was so overpowering that she felt dizzy and suffocated.

The blood dripping from the severed heads of goats and pigeons filled the ground on which the twelve Chinese occultists were chanting and dancing.

She took some pictures with her phone camera, and video recorded the proceedings. She realized that if she stayed any longer, she would faint and would be caught, and the thought of being caught sent a shiver up her spine.

She quietly retreated and managed to return to her camp.

She heaved a sigh of relief at being back safely at her tent and began to think about her next course of action.

She knew immediately that she had unearthed a secret supernatural conspiracy but could not understand about its implications. So, she decided that she should go to Ved and Malti to tell what she saw, and then together they would be able to decide what to do next.

Ved, Malti, and Manu were shocked to hear Priya's story. Ved understood the implications of what Priya had just narrated. He expected something like this would happen but was still taken by surprise listening to Priya's findings.

They decided to inform the Chief of Security for the Kumbh Mela, Deputy Commissioner of Police (DCP) Prakash Pandey about the entire incident.

It was early next morning when the four of them met the DCP, and Priya described what she saw to the DCP.

The DCP organized a raid team immediately and all of them went to the site where the occult ritual was carried out earlier that night.

They found the remains of the ritual, but the Chinese priests had left the place. Two Chinese men monitoring the control room were duly arrested, and all the equipment were taken into police custody.

Now, the bigger problem before them was how to apprehend the 12 Chinese occultists!

The police retrieved the mugshots of the 12 Chinese occultists from Priya's recordings, and sent out a BOLO (look out notice) to all security personnel and undercover agents deployed at the Mela.

All their efforts to spot the Chinese priests yielded no results. A severe sense of tension grew amongst the Mela Management Committee members as they had no clue as to what these Chinese saboteurs were planning to do.

Although Ved had a fair idea, he could not tell the others about it, as they would never believe about things that occurred at a paranormal level.

Ved, Malti, and Manu took Priya into confidence and described in detail about the sabotage plans by the Chinese occultists, and their intent to grab the controls of the management of our planet and the eco system by hijacking the Hiranya-Garbha ceremony for raising the Kamandal and the Amrit.

Priya was dumbfounded listening to the things that Ved, Malti, and Manu had just told her. This was something out of the Hollywood movie 'Avatar', but only this one was for real.

Ved, Malti, and Manu were elevated beings with clairvoyant powers, and they finally managed to track down the twelve Chinese perpetrators. They located each one of them – one each at the 12 Akharas inside the Mela campus. But not in the real sense of the term – they were no longer the same faces as the real ones. The Chinese perpetrators had now possessed the Akhara heads and became them, and hence were invisible.

And now Ved realized what these Chinese occultists were up to.

Veda remembered that when they tried to apprehend the Chinese priests at the Akhara camps with the help of the DCP and his team, they were too late. They had disappeared.

To investigate the sequence of events Ved, Malti, and Manu sat for an emergency meditation session at the site of the Maha Yajna. They sat at three tips of a triangular shaped platform with the SRI YANTRA tool (also a configuration of triangles) at the center.

It was a Tantrik procedure to look at the cosmic vibrations around the Kumbh Mela, and into the evil vibrations caused by the Chinese perpetrators.

Like in a crystal gazing session, the Sri Yantra showed them the sequence of the events that would take place during the auspicious day of the Shahi Snan, and during the Maha Yajna to raise the Kamandal and the Amrit.

Now they became aware, as to what was expected during the Maha Yajna at the Hiranya-Garbh. But they still had no idea what to do to avert the conspiracy.

They decided to keep a strict but discrete vigil on the twelve Akhara heads.

And soon it was noticeable that the heads of the Akharas behaving in an abnormal manner, and as if they were not accustomed to the lives of a Akhara head. They repeatedly faltered during their routine role as Akhara head, and as time progressed it became quite clear that they were pretenders – not the real Akhara heads.

The sadhus of the Akharas were puzzled as to why the Akhara heads were behaving so differently!

Later they realized the truth that the Akhara heads were subjected to some sort of Tantrism, and hence they behaved the way they did.

Not knowing what they should do, Ved, Malti, and Manu once again conducted a mini Yajna throughout the night till the wee hours of the Shahi Snan the next day, at the site of the Hiranya-Garbha where the Maha Kumbh Maha Yajna was to be held, to invoke Mahavatar Babaji, the Mountain Man, and all others who protected the Mt. Kailash and the Shaivik wisdom of spirituality.

They all appeared in flesh and blood at the mini Yajna.

The mini Yajna was continued in their presence, and the Hiranya-Garbha was now fortified by the presence of divine powers.

While the preparations and arrangements for the Kumbh Maha Yajna was in full swing, most of the other sadhus and priest were completely unaware of the Chinese conspiracy.

The next day evening at 6 pm about hundred odd sadhus, priests, and rishis from the hidden caves of the Himalayas gathered at the site of the Hiranya-Garbh to perform the Maha Kumbh Maha Yajna.

Nobody from the regular crowd of visitors to the Mela had any knowledge about the Maha Yajna.

The Akhara heads – all twelve of them, possessed by the Chinese priests also mingled amidst the congregation for the Maha Yajna.

Ved, Malti, and Manu along with Priya and DCP Pandey too joined the group with a team of special commando force keeping a strict vigil on each of the twelve Akhara heads (Chinese priests).

The Maha Yajna proceedings started on a sedate note and continued smoothly till about midnight.

The Vedic chanting, the sound of the mantras, the flames of the Yajna fire leaping into the sky at the resounding utterance of the word "SWAHA" each time after the priests and sadhus performing the Yajna poured ghee (clarified butter) into the fire, and the numerous other Vedic rites performed at the Yajna created an electrifying charged atmosphere that permeated across the skies.

And while the next phase of the Maha Yajna was about to be conducted, things began to happen that disrupted the proceedings. They were small incidents initially. They do happen sometimes. But it was not before long, that the priests and the sadhus realized that the light and sound energy emanating from the flames were slowly turning from bright golden colour to pale yellowish initially, and then to darker greyish!

The smell of the air which was earlier filled with that of 'Panchamrit' and other fresh 'Havan-Samagri' was now becoming more like a bitter stench.

Panchamrit – a concoction of Yoghurt, Ghee, Honey, Milk, and Sugar, used during a Havan Yajna (holy fire ritual).

Havan Samagri – are Ayurvedic herbs, spices, such as, black sesame, barley, camphor, rose petals, sandal wood powder, and a variety of incense.

And then out of nowhere, a strange smoky transparent globe emerged, and in the blink of an eye, engulfed the entire Hiranya-Garbha inside it!!!

The Yajna fires slowly died down, and the proceedings of the Maha Yajna came to an abrupt halt.

The Chinese occultists were the first ones to be shocked at the turn of events. They had their own plans for sabotaging the event, but now they realized that they were outsmarted! But nothing made any sense to them, as every indication pointed to an act of a celestial warfare.

Then they realized that it was the spirit of Yaku Xi who had hijacked the event, including themselves.

Apparently, this circular object was a globe shielded by an extraordinary medium of elements that were beyond the realms of the planetary system.

The globe radiated a very powerful force that repelled the force of gravity of the Earth, and quickly ballooned upward beyond the limits of the Earth's gravity, and floated there.

All the participants of the Maha Kumbh Maha Yajna found themselves captured inside this alien space that was outside of the elemental configuration of the cosmos.

The rishis, the priests, and the sadhus realized that the Maha Yajna was sabotaged, and they were all kidnapped by some unknown supernatural power.

It was not long before that they saw the fearsome face of Yaku Xi the sorcerer of the 11th century – his dilated face radiating across the surface of the crystal globe in which they were held captive.

The twelve Chinese perpetrators who were inside the Hiranya-Garbha tried their best to convey to the spirit of Yaku Xi that they were not the Akhara heads but were the Chinese occultists, but Yaku Xi laughed at them saying that he didn't need them anymore.

It was a stroke of fate that Ved, Malti, Manu, and Priya found themselves out of the Hiranya-Garbha at that very moment as DCP Pandey took them away to verify some information that they received from the Chinese men who were operating the computer room inside the cave that Priya had discovered.

The two Chinese computer operators confessed that there was an elaborate plan to sabotage the Maha Yajna by the twelve Chinese occultists with the help of the spirit of Yaku Xi. They provided explicit details of the ancient scriptures that these twelve had stolen from a Buddhist monastery in Tawang, Arunachal Pradesh, with which they were able to revoke the spirit of Yaku Xi.

The information shocked Ved as he realized the implications of the eminent dangers that the entire ecosystem faced – something that had never happened before.

It became quite clear by then, that the spirit of Yaku Xi, by cleverly manipulating the twelve Chinese priests was seeking his own immortality to become the master of the universe by dethroning Lord Shiva at the Kailash Parvat.

Ved realized then, that the situation had taken a whole new turn and it was no longer a situation that could be handled at human physical level.

What followed next at the gross level was that the auspicious 'Surya uday (Sunrise) for the 'Shahi Snan' didn't occur.

The millions who had gathered for the Shahi Snan waited for the 'Suryudaya' to happen, but little did they know that a deadly sinister event was manifesting at that very moment right there – unseen to them.

A battle manifested at a cosmic level between the army of the keepers of the Himalayan tradition, and the spirit of Yaku Xi with his powers of black magic.

But all their efforts to penetrate Yaku Xi's globe met with failure.

Only a few people apart from Ved, Malti, Manu, and Priya, were privy to the paranormal tussle that was taking place at an astral sphere.

At that moment, at behest of the Mountain Man, Ved, Malti, Manu and a few others began to revive the Maha Yajna afresh at the same site of the Hiranya-Garbha to invoke Lord Shiva.

As the Maha Yajna progressed, multiple waves of cosmic energy were created. The people who came for the Shahi Snan too joined the Maha Yajna in large numbers praying for the 'Surya uday' (Sunrise) to happen.

The intensity of the freshly performed Maha Yajna created a new plane at the astral level that resulted in the appearance of the Deity of 'Hari-Hara' – an enjoined avatar of Gods Lord Shiva and Lord Vishnu.

Mahavatar Babaji sat at the center of an octagon while the eight other Maha Rishis sat at the base of each face of the octagon. Every base of the octagon formed a triangle converging at the central point where Mahavatar Babaji sat.

It was a spectacular site where each of the twelve Maha Rishis were directly facing Mahavatar Babaji's face, meaning that Mahavatar Babaji sat facing in twelve different directions all at the same time!

The third eye of each of the twelve Maha Rishis beamed a bright blue ray of light into the third eye of Mahavatar Babaji, thus forming twelve triangles by the rays of the light beamed by the Maha Rishis.

Then the twelve triangles formed by the beams began to lift to a further higher plane, and then it started to swirl slowly forming a vertical triangle.

Then the tip of the vertical triangle transformed into a hazy cloud of smoke, and from amidst the smoke appeared an enjoined face of Lord Shiva and Lord Vishnu. This was a spectacle that could not be described in words.

The sky resonated with sounds of chanting of the words "Jai Jai Hari-Har" as the conjoined form of 'Hari and Har' became larger and larger and spread out across the entire sky.

And as the enjoined face of Hari-Har engulfed the entire space, the satellite globe created by Yaku Xi was forced down towards the ground by the intense pressure created by the expanding shape of the conjoined faces of Lord Shiva and Lord Vishnu.

And in no time, the globe was forced to re-enter Earth's gravitational pull. Now the globe was sucked back on to the ground.

The moment Yaku Xi's globe touched the ground, it came into the ambit of the Maha Yajna that was in progress and it cracked open the globe releasing a huge ball of fire into the sky. And in the flame, the spirit of Yaku Xi was burnt to ashes. A nauseating stink pervaded the atmosphere for a brief period of time.The captives were now free at the ground level.

DCP Pandey and his team of commandos took all of them into their protection, and the twelve heads of the Akharas, aka the Chinese priests into their own custody.

Ved, Malti, Manu and the others were so absorbed in the activity at the astral level that little did they realize that eight days had already passed by. Time had stood still for everybody at the Mela too!

The Maha Yajna at ground level once again achieved its peak and towards the wee hours on the eighth day, three streams of water burst out from the ground surface with a ferocious force. The three streams then collided with each other and spiraled upward just like a twister tornado. The water spiraled upward reached a height of about two hundred feet.

There was a dazzling aura of rainbow as the water fountain furrowed into the sky, which gradually became a blurry fog not visible with clarity to a normal human eye.

Just as all this was happening, Mahavatar Babaji appeared from the sky and held in his hand, a shining Kamandal from the tip of the water fountain.

Thus, the Maha Yajna of the Maha Kumbh Mela was completed with the retrieval of the Kamandal, and the 'Suryudaya' (Sunrise) for the 'Shahi Snan' which duly took place for the thousands of people who had waited for the holy dip.

This was the moment, all the participants of the Maha Yajna had waited for, with abated breath.

This was the moment when the Gods and His gross creation (the Humans and Prakriti - Nature) came together on planet earth.

The sound of the conch shells filled the sky amidst an amazing divine fragrance and showers of floral petals from the sky.

They were all there showering blessings from the sky- The Saptarshi (the Maha-Rishis), Prajapati, all the Devtas led by Indra, Lord Vishnu with spouse Goddess Lakshmi, and Rishi Narada, Lord Shiva with spouse goddess Parvati, and Lord Brahma with spouse Goddess Saraswati. Lord Ganesh and Bajrangbali Hanuman too appeared for this grand occasion.

It was a sight to behold, when the fountain that carried the Kamandal at it's tip, was picked up by Mahavatar Babaji.

Then Mahavatar Babaji rose to the sky atop the Mt. Kailash and sprinkled the Amrit from the Kamandal on to the tip of Mt. Kailash, thereby infusing 'Prana' (seeds of life force energies) once again on the planet Earth!

Thus, life on planet Earth and its cosmic governance was sustained at the Mt. Kailash, after the successful completion of the 144th Maha Kumbh Mela at the Triveni Sangam,

Prayagraj, where the Gods and the humans mingled to make the 'Amrit-Manthan' happen by overcoming the evil, darkness and ignorance!

***

Chapter IX
AASTIKA - THE BELIEVERS

Unknown to most of the eighty-ninety million people who visit the Kumbh Mela and the ritual of Shahi Snan (the pious dip in the holy waters), there are at least a thousand Himalayan monks who come out of their self-imposed isolation to take part in the Kumbh Mela.

They are referred to as the 'Aastika' –The Believers. They are a self-realized, evolved lot, who accessed into the higher plane of the Shradhhashram – Gyanganj.

These Himalayan sadhus are both Shivites (devotees of Lord Shiva), and also Vaishnavites (devotees of Lord Vishnu).

They are devotees of extreme surrender to their faith and hence live a life of complete abstinence from any kind of obligations of 'Samsara' and are free from any bondage. No laws or rules bound them and they spend prolonged hours in deep meditation, their consciousness floating in the cosmic consciousness and awareness of their 'Aradhya' (one who they worship).

Nobody knows where they live - unseen and unheard for years together. They seem to possess superior consciousness with extraordinary levels of perception and extraordinary abilities.

They are like an army of elite warriors who protect the Himalayan eco system - the apex center of governance of our planet.

Hence it is quite natural, that this band of Aastikas (believers) were active during the Kumbh Mela to oversee a hassle-free conclusion to the rituals performed – that of churning out of the Kamandal.

A long lineage of such sadhus under the Avatars of 'God-descent' Mahavatar Babaji, Adi Shankaracharya, and many others adorn the canvas of Hindu spiritualism.

Names such as Lahiri Mahashaya, Swami Pranavananda, Swami Vishuddhananda, Swami Sri Yukteswar Giri, Hamsa Swami Kevalananda, Swami Hariharananda, Neem Karoli Baba, Paramhamsa Yogananda, and their lineages provided a rich spiritual heritage of wisdom for the Hindu faith across the centuries.

Swami Rama, another protégée from the Himalayan school of spiritualism was known as the master of the Himalayan tradition. He had an ashram at the beautiful Tarakeshwar Temple near Lansdowne town in the Garhwal district of Uttarakhand in India.

The sole emphasis on spiritualism rather than on religious leanings, make the Himalayan school of spiritualism universal, and outside the shackles of any religion. The only path they follow is one that connected the 'Atman' (soul) to the 'Parmatman' – the divine source of the soul.

Spiritualism is a path taken by rebels who seeks out truths of the universe by themselves. They discover the truths and the realities beyond the gross physical world by walking the spiritual path.

And to do that, they isolate themselves from the society and the dualities of Maya (illusion) and transcend at the soul level in a meditative state to communicate with the microcosmic universal wisdom.

Spiritualism is pure science, and the practitioner perceives wisdom at a much-elevated level of perception.

An elevated level of perception is possible when the practitioner is able to expand his brain activity to a far larger level, and when the mind has transcended from gross physical level to the subtle level.

In such a state the practitioner can access universal cosmic wisdom from the infinite plane of consciousness.

Such wisdom thus accessed, are free from Maya or duality, and are pure and absolute.

It is akin to a scientist who relentlessly dedicates his life to his research in his lab, cutting himself off from the outer world to remain focused in his research. He is immersed in a world away from the Samsara, and in a plane created by the subject of his research.

Like a scientist, a spiritual practitioner too isolates himself from the world of physical illusion in his quest for the truths of the universal wisdom.

There are no rules and ritualistic bindings for those on the spiritual path, unlike those followed in the religious places.

Spiritualism doesn't have any dos and don'ts.

Spiritualism provides freedom to explore the distant horizon like the migratory birds and fly thousands of miles to seek out their destination.

A soul is free from the expressions of any kind, and hence is not limited only to the knowledge and wisdom gathered by the five sensory organs. One can see things with the eyes which may not be the truth. One may hear things that might be false, because our sensory organs are always subject to the influence of the mind.

But the knowledge acquired at a non-dual level of perception (when the mind is not influenced by Maya) is the real truth.

Spiritualism is universally human, and unbiased. Hence spiritualism is essentially a seeker's domain which elevates the person to a higher level which is described as 'Self Realization', akin to God realization.

Hence the Hindu 'Sloka' (hymn)–

"Chidanandam Roopam Shivoham Shivoham!"

It means that we are akin to God, and the realization of the same takes us to the level of God.

Spiritualism also is a process of self-upgradation (purification) – both at psychic level and physical level.

A person with a flawed mindset can never perceive the truths of the self, and that of God and the universal wisdom.

Hence spiritualism advocates the practice of the following eight basic principles -

- Tan Shuddhi – a cleansed/healthy *body*
- Man Shuddhi – a pure and positive *mindset*
- Bhav Shuddhi – pure *thoughts* generated by the mind
- Vivek Shuddhi – creating a pure *moral conscience*
- Vichaar Shuddhi – pure, and unbiased *decisions* generated from the thoughts
- Baak Shuddhi – pure speech

- Karam Shuddhi – good *Karma* out of the good Vichaars (decisions)
- Dharam Shuddhi – a *righteous path* out of the good Karma

The playground of the mind, where a person nurses millions of thoughts is also a fertile breeding ground for negativities due to the illusory whims of the six 'Arishadvarga' (desires/passions) which are:

- Kama (lust)
- Krodh (anger)
- Lobh (greed)
- Mada (arrogance)
- Moh (attachment)
- Matsarya (jealousy)

Hence, it is important for a seeker of truth to be able to tame their minds and to dwell at a plane that is free from the claws of the above six vulnerabilities, to allow them to focus on the absolute truth sans any duality of Maya.

Himalayan spirituality is timeless and hence flourishes amidst the manifold diversity of human belief systems.

There is no restriction, and no one questions each other in the Himalayan school of spirituality. Numerous streams of spirituality thrive in the Himalayan region, amidst the abode of prevailing divinity.

Only a person with extremely strong intent can survive the arduous endurance of going without food for days, and also harsh environment of the Himalayas.

Hence only those with a strong determination can go on to become a Himalayan Sadhu.

Like passing from one grade of school to a higher-grade, year after year, in life too, mastering each level of the

Ashtanga Yoga from Yama, Niyama …. up to the Dharana, Dhyana, and Samadhi level enables one to become a 'Sadhak', and to become eligible to become a 'Swami' – a designation like the PhD, that separates one from the rest of the others who dwell in a of lower plane of self.

Hence, they are a revered lot.

'Sadhna' is a Sanskrit word which means dedicated, disciplined, and relentless pursuance of spiritualism.

The word 'Sadhu', or a 'Sadhak', is one who is engaged in 'Sadhna'. The more acute the Sadhna, the more accomplished the Sadhak, or the Sadhu.

And to begin with, only those accomplished souls qualify to pursue such high level of Sadhna in the Himalayas who have acquired a specified higher level of spiritual consciousness from their earlier past lives. Hence, our life is a spiritual journey from zero level of awareness to a complete level of awareness at the end of the journey of the soul, after thousands of lifetimes and births.

The good thing is that such accomplished sadhus usually share their wisdom with other seekers, and some of these sadhaks become gurus to guide the common folk to unveil the truths to hasten their journey of the soul.

These gurus are rare to locate, as they do not seek recognition or publicity.

It is said that these Gurus spot their 'Shishya' (students) and take them under their tutelage, and not the other way round. And hence it's only a very few deserving ones who find a genuine guru in their life!

And these Himalayan Sadhus also come out of their caves in large numbers during the Kumbh Mela to become a part of the congregation of the millions during the Mela to share with them their lifestyle, discuss their philosophies and wisdom, and answer queries that are put to them by curious seekers.

The sadhus usually draw a lot of attention from the visitors of the Mela because of their strange behavior, and their attire, specially the Naga Sadhus, and the Aghoris.

Varieties of sects of sadhus come to the Mela in groups (Akharas), and camp at their designated location inside the Mela premises.

Some of these sadhus perform miraculous yogic postures, and acts - such as walking barefoot on fire, walking on water, taking Samadhi underground and staying for days without oxygen, some of them staying afloat in the air levitating, and many more such acts to entertain the visitors.

And amidst such entertainment, there are also teaching sessions on the art of Tantrism, Srividya, how to use and read the Sri Yantra, and the art of Yoga, and Yoga-Sadhna etc.

In the context of our modern times, the mysticism of the Himalayan spiritualism has caught the fancy of a large number of westerners, who come in doves to find answers to their un-satiated illusions of their minds.

Many such seekers become monks – some become followers of Buddhism, and while many others take to the life of Hindu Sadhus to find their mental peace in the Himalayan spiritual sanctuary.

They find their answers to questions like – "Who Am I?", "Why Am I?", "What's the purpose of my life?", etc.

This universal abode of spirituality is a place where everyone is welcome from any corner of the world without any prejudice.

Now Ved, Malti, and Manu too joined the illustrious ranks of the guide angels of the Himalayan tradition, just like the Mountain Man and the others to become inspirational motivators, and teachers to guide the humanity in the right direction.

****

Chapter X

IN THE FOOTPRINTS OF THE HIMALAYAN MASTERS -

Mahavatar BABAJI

The legend of the Himalayas, Mahavatar of Babaji walks the human trail even today after thousands of years as an Avatar of Lord Shiva.

A deathless Yogi, Babaji attained deathlessness at the age of 16 near the famous Himalayan site of pilgrimage- Badrinath shrine.

Babaji still roams the spiritual abode of the Himalayas, teaching and guiding humanity and seekers of spiritualism, and most importantly, as a protector of the Himalayan abode of spiritualism.

Many lucky ones get to see him in flesh and blood from time to time, and often Babaji appears in one's dream to provide guidance and assistance to carry out their dispensations.

The deathless Babaji is an Avatar who descended on Earth just as many others such as Lord Krishna, Gautam Buddha, Lord Rama, and Patanjali, and a lineage of Rishi Agastya from South India.

The story goes that Babaji was born in the year 203 AD on the 30th November in a small village now known as Parangipettal in the state of Tamil Nadu in South India.

He was named as Nagraj with reference to the Kundalini energies in the human body, represented by a coiled snake that sat at the base of one's 'Muladhara Chakra' (root chakra).

Born to a priest family in a small village, Nagraj was also a descent of the famous priest lineage of the Nambudri Brahmins who are known as the priests for the most revered Vishnu temple at Badrinath in the Himalayas.

His father was the priest of the main temple, or 'Koil' in Tamil. This temple was dedicated to Lord Shiva and was located barely 17 Kms from the famous Chidambaram Temple in Tamil Nadu.

The Chidambaram Temple hosts the most charismatic image of Lord Shiva's Nataraj – the cosmic dancer, under a roof covered by more than 2260 gold tiles held in place by 72,000 odd gold nails.

Being the son of the head priest, Nagraj grew up in an environment of spirituality right from his childhood.

Nagraj was barely 5 years of age when he was kidnapped by an Afghani national and was taken on a boat to Calcutta (present Kolkata) and was sold to a wealthy 'Jamindar' (landlord) as a slave. He was among many other such young boys who were sold across the state of West Bengal.

The Jamindar's wife noticed that this young boy was quite different from the others and was quiet, aloof, and meditated a lot. He was not interested in the usual things that other boys of his age were interested in, and he was of no use as a worker.

And after discussing this with her husband, she decided to release him, and asked him to go back to his home.

Nagraj told her that he didn't want to go back home, and that he wanted to go to the Himalayas.

It was quite ironical that Nagraj's destiny took him to the Himalayas where he belonged; unlike many other seekers who had to renounce their familial ties abruptly to come to the Himalayas in search of Nirvana.

That was at the age of five when Babaji headed for the Himalayas, and with the support of a group of sanyasis, he disappeared in the mountains.

Later when he appeared again, he became known as the 'Mrintyunjayee Babaji' – who conquered death at the age of 16. And he forever retained the same youthful look of a 16 year-old!

It has been only recently – during the last sixty years that a lot of facts about Babaji surfaced when some ancient scriptures written on palm leaves were discovered near the town of Pondicherry (the present Pudduchery).

Many renowned saints and yogis have mentioned about Babaji in their memoirs like Paramhans Yogananda (Autobiography of a Yogi book, 1946). His Guru Swami Yukteswar Giri also wrote extensively about Babaji.

Baba Hari Dass identified Babaji as the Hariakhan Baba who appeared in the town Ranikhet towards the end of the 19th century.

Swami Satyeswarananda described his incredible encounters with Babaji (1984).

The theosophists Reverend C.W. Leadbeater and Annie Besant also described their encounter with Babaji in person, some sixty-five years ago.

Adi Shankaracharya:

Adi Shankaracharya (788-820 AD), the father of the Hinduism post the beginning of the Christian calendar, was a direct disciple of Mahavatar Babaji, mentioned several references to a close connect between Babaji and Jesus Christ- the son of God (ref. Autobiography of a Yogi).

Adi Shankaracharya, one of the most prominent names of Hindu philosophy and spiritualism was given 'Diksha' (initiation) by Mahavatar Babaji. He was born in the year 788AD at a place called Kalady to parents Aryamba and Sivaguru. Initially, he was mentored by his Guru Govinda Bhagavatpada, and was later initiated by Mahavatar Babaji into Kriya Kundalini Yoga. Thus, Govindapad was the 'Shiksha-Guru' (education and life sciences), and Mahavatar Babaji was his 'Diksha-Guru' (Yoga initiation into spiritual sciences). This was later testified by Swami Yogananda, Sri Yukteswar (Swami Yogananda's Guru), Swami Kebalananda, and Swami Keshabananda that Lahiri Mahasay, a great saint disciple of Mahavatar Babaji, spoke of Babaji being Adi Shankaracharya's spiritual Guru.

Adi Shankaracharya was one of the most influential philosophers of the Hindu religion and was responsible in bringing about several reforms towards discarding numerous superstitious beliefs and practices.

He was also responsible for systematizing the religion and its practices by projecting Hinduism as not just a religion, but a Vedantic way of Life. His philosophy on Advaita Vedanta that emphasizes on non-duality is still considered profound with respect to our modern scientific mindset.

As a result of his writings, debates, and travels far and wide, several immoral practices in Hindu temples were eliminated, and several other demoralizing sects of Hinduism such as Buddhism practically relocated from India. With his clear and rational monistic philosophy, he was able to motivate many Hindu thinkers for centuries thereafter.

Sant Kabir:

Sant Kabir was another reformer saint influenced by Mahavatar Babaji during the 15th -16th century.

The versatility of spiritualism in the Himalayan abode is reflected by acceptance of faiths beyond the boundaries of any religion, and Sant Kabir – the great Saint Poet is a grand example of the same.

Sant Kabir was a reformer who opened the doors of his sect to both Hindus, and to Muslims, by preaching a monistic conception of God and advised against idol worship. His reforms were a synthetic reaction to the challenges of Islam. He was instrumental in bringing harmony between the factional Hindus and Muslims by adhering to an ascetic life instead of fighting for the religious gospels that shackled their perceptive growth.

He taught his pupils to eat vegetarian food, and to avoid any kind of intoxicants.

Mahavatar Babaji initiated Sant Kabir during the 15th century, encouraged his emphasis on 'Naada Meditation' (meditation on the divine sound of Lord Shiva's Damru).

The concept of sound vibration energies playing a major role in the sustenance of our planet is described in the verse

–*"Naada dheenam, jagata sarvam"* – meaning, the entire Jagat (our planet) survives due to the sound vibrations of Lord Shiva's Damru.

Sant Kabir's poems and 'sayings' have been collected by one of his followers in a book called the 'Bijaka', which reflected on his path - 'Kabirpanthi', in both ascetic, and householder sections of our society.

Lahiri Mahasaya:

Lahiri Mahasaya (1828-1895), a prominent disciple of Mahavatar Babaji, was initiated into the art of Kriya Yoga in the year 1861. This was a period in the last half of the 19th century that Babaji was highly active on his mission to spread the art of Kriya Yoga – a yogic procedure that helped erase one's bad Karma by a process of inner cleansing of the self at psychic and soul level.

Lahiri Mahasaya lived a normal familial life and showed that a seeker can achieve self-realization and Moksha even by living in Samsarik (amidst the human eco system) conditions.

Thus, Lahiri Mahasaya initiated hundreds of seekers into Kriya Yoga with the blessings of Mahavatar Babaji, and is described in Swami Satyeswarananda's famous book – 'Lahiri Mahasaya - The Father Of Kriya Yoga''. The book also traces the lineage of disciples who were taught by Lahiri Mahasaya. He affirms that Mahavatar Babaji himself helped and continues to help those who practiced the art of Kriya Yoga faithfully.

Thus, the system of dedicating any Kriya at the start of practice, to Mahavatar Babaji began by chanting the words –*"Om Kriya Babaji Namoh Om"*

It is said that such dedication to Babaji implied a direct participation of Mahavatar Babaji during the practice of Kriya Yoga.

Sri Yukteswar Maharaj Giri:

Sri Yukteswar Maharaj Giri (1855-1936), an enlightened prodigy of Lahiri Mahasaya, was highly instrumental in spreading the art and sciences of Kriya Yoga in India and also beyond the Indian shores to the far away countries. His book *'The Holy Science'*, and his establishments of numerous discourse centers across the country attracted thousands of pupils. His most famous pupil was none other than Yogananda Paramhansa, whom he sent to the USA to spread the sciences of Kriya Yoga.

Later Yogananda Paramhansa's book – 'The Autobiography of a Yogi' took the world of spiritualism by storm and changed the lives of millions across the world!

Paramhansa Yogananda:

Paramhansa Yogananda (1893-1952) was sent to America in the year 1920 by his Guru Sri Yukteswar Maharaj to introduce Yoga based philosophies of eastern mysticism in the West.

There were several stories of how Yogananda, who didn't even know how to speak in English miraculously began to speak fluent English, and how he was instrumental in influencing thousands of his Christian brothers in the US to learn the sciences of Kriya Yoga – thanks to Babaji's special grace.

He established the famous Encinitas Hermitage – The Self Realization Fellowship (SRF) Ashram at Los Angeles,

California – the building jutting out like a white 'Ocean-Liner' hovering over the vast blue ocean, made possible through the generosity of American disciples, and businessmen whose newfound harmony of faith in Yogananda's sciences, and who found time for their daily Sunrise Kriya Yoga at his ashram.

Yogananda was not even aware that the hermitage building was being constructed by his followers, as during that time, he was busy in India establishing his Yogoda Sat Sangh Society at Dakshineswar, West Bengal, and the Yogoda School at Ranchi located in the state of Jharkhand, India.

Yogananda ji trained over a hundred thousand followers into the art of Kriya Yoga, including the likes of Mahatma Luther Burbank.

Yogananda attained Maha Samadhi in the year 1952 – a Yogi's conscious exit from our 'bhoutic' world (physical world) to merge into the limitlessness of the subtle cosmic world.

Yogi S.A.A. Ramaiah:

Yogi S.A.A. Ramaiah was yet another renowned yogi blessed and initiated by Mahavatar Babaji and influenced by Himalayan spiritualism. The son of a wealthy businessman in South India, he was a deeply spiritual young man, who graduated in Geology from Madras University. He had then proceeded to the USA for pursuing his post graduate studies when he was diagnosed with bone tuberculosis.

The story of Ramaiah's miraculous recovery is an astonishing tribute to several spiritual gurus and avataras, namely Mahavatar Babaji, Shirdi Sai Baba, and Mowna Swami, a devotee of Sai Baba.

One day, unable to bear the pain and facing the imminent torment of an eluding death, Ramaiah decided to end his life by holding his breath. It was at that moment, that he heard the soothing voice of Babaji asking him not to end his life, and instead asked him to give him his life. The words of Babaji had a mesmerizing effect on him and he took a deep long breath and decided to surrender his life to Babaji.

What followed, was a rapid and miraculous process of healing that took the entire medical fraternity by surprise. Ramaiah was completely cured of his bone tuberculosis!

And in the following few days, Ramaiah saw in his vision, the sight of Babaji limping and walking past him. It was anybody's guess as to what must have happened – that Babaji took Ramaiah's tuberculosis unto himself to honor the act of Ramaiah's surrender to him.

Later Babaji himself initiated Ramaiah into various techniques of Kriya Yoga near Badrinath around 1955, where Babaji's Himalayan cave was located.

Further to his initiation at Badrinath, Ramaiah blossomed into a Yogi of prominence, and went on to hone his healing skills by joining GS Medical College, Bombay.

Hence, he learnt to apply his wisdom of spiritual healing in tandem with the techniques of modern physiotherapy, with great success.

Swami Rama:

Of the most recent ones from the Himalayan belt, one who standouts the most is Swami Rama who was also being decorated with the title of 'The Master of the Himalayan Tradition'.

Born in the year 1925, Swami Rama was known to be born out of a boon given to his mother by the great Himalayan saint 'Bangali Baba', and later Swami Rama himself became a disciple of Bangali Baba.

Swami Rama in his autobiography 'Living with the Himalayan Masters' narrates his spiritual journey in the Himalayas, and about his numerous associations of several highly evolved saints.

One such sadhaka was the Shankarcharya of Jyotirmoya Peetham located on the way to Badrinath in the Himalayas.

He lived in a cave and ate only germinated grams with a little bit of salt. He taught Swami Rama about Sri Vidya, the highest of paths, followed only by accomplished Sanskrit scholars – one that joins Raja Yoga, Kundalini Yoga, Bhakti Yoga, and Advaita Vedanta.

Sri Vidya, and Madhu Vidya are spiritual practices that are known to only a few advanced practitioners.

Swami Rama wrote more than a dozen books and had many American and European disciples.

He also set up 'The Himalayan Institute' located on a 400-acre campus in the hills of Pocono Mountains in northern Pennsylvania, USA.

Dev Raha Baba:

The ageless Yogi Dev Raha Baba was a regular visitor in the Himalayan belt and was a mystery unto himself. Some speculate that he could have been anywhere between 150-200 years of age when Swami Rama met him. He was known to live on Machans (wooden platform made on a tree used by hunters as observatory), and he used to peek out from the hidden Machans to talk to his disciples.

Sadhu Sundar Singh:

Sadhu Sundar Singh, a young Sikh boy one day suddenly left his home for the Himalayas at the behest of a vision that urged him not to waste time and go to pursue his purpose. Apparently, the person in his vision was no other than Jesus Christ!

The Mystery of 'Siddhashrama':

Deep into the Himalayas, near the Kailash Parvat (Mt. Kailash – the abode of Lord Shiva) there is believed to be this mystical hermitage called the 'Siddhashrama'.

Literally Siddhashrama translates into – 'Siddha' means attaining self-realization, and 'Shrama' is short form for an 'Ashrama' – a spiritual hermitage.

Siddhashram is also popularly known as Gyanganj, which means a place of wisdom.

This is a place where highly evolved yogis, sadhus, sanyasis, monks, and yetis dwell amidst a number of immortal souls from the yester Yugas thus forming a society of enlightened divinity.

Located in a secret place near the Mansarovar lake and the Kailash Parvat, this hermitage is believed to be specially blessed by Lord Shiva and Goddess Parvati.

Many siddha yogis, yoginis, apsaras (angels), saints are believed to be in a state of deep meditation in order to achieve salvation at the feet of Lord Shiva or Lord Vishnu.

It is believed that only those who have attained a certain level of spiritual awareness are able to gain access to this place, and the place hides itself from ordinary humans seeking information about the place.

Swami Rama, and Swami Vishuddhananda Paramhansa talked about Gyanganj in public. Both were taken to Gyanganj by their gurus and were asked to do sadhna there for many many years.

Folklore has it that many immortal rishis and saints from yester Yugas, such as Maharshi Vashista, Vishwamitra, Rishi Atri, Maha Yogi Goraknath, Pulatsya, Kanda, Pitamaha Bhishma, Adi Shankaracharya, Kripacharya and many others are seen to be wandering around in their physical form at Gyanganj, and also conducting Satsang and giving sermons!

Needless to say, that Siddhashram, aka Gyanganj exists at an elevated level of perception, and on a higher plane, which is for all practical purpose, is the doorway to heaven – to achieve liberation.

***

Chapter XI
PANORAMA OF HINDU FAITH – AN AMAZING CANVAS OF TEMPLES, GODS AND GODESSES

Faith, per se, is something that is a very personal thing and manifests from one's heart. It's something that a person builds during the passage of his life, and it becomes a part of his belief system.

Yet, most of the time, most of us accept a superficial faith that our society thrusts upon us, as a part of the traditional religious protocols. Such faiths are no more than social alignments adhering to a compliance system, and they crumble under the slightest pressure of tough situations during the course of our life.

Faith is not a fancy piece of choice to ordain the self. It's a far deeper inner consciousness that evolves ever so slowly over decades, and when it does, it awakens the strength of one's spirituality.

In Treta Yuga, in the epic of Ramayana, Hanuman aka, Bajrangbali plays the role of a devotee of Lord Rama, who is an Avatar of Lord Vishnu. Here, the character of Hanuman portrays an epitome of the highest level of 'Bhakti' (devoted love), faith and trust for his beloved God Lord Rama. His unparalleled Bhakti (faith + trust = Bhakti) empowered him with the ability to perform impossible tasks and showed that the power of one's Bhakti can manifest a Shakti (power and ability) that can overcome the impossible.

One's faith is much more than being a believer on the protocols of a religion, it is Bhakti (faith + trust), emanating from the core of one's inner consciousness that creates a very powerful association with one's God.

And once we are discussing God and our faith, there is no other factor between the two – 'the believer' and the 'believed', not even any religion.

The faith in a religion is an indirect approach to faith in God. There is a lot of squabbling amidst the religious houses, as can be seen in our society – each religion enforcing its dictates to its followers which has led to breaking up of religions into numerous newer segments in almost all religions, leading to disruption of one's faith.

The religions have strict protocols vis-à-vis one's moral code of conduct and practices. The House of God in each religion is called by different names as per the names of their Gods.

They offer prayers as per the main scripture of their religion, wear different robes, and so on so forth.

That brings us to the question of God – Who is the God we pray and have our faith in - an unseen superior consciousness, or a superior being with Godly attributes, such as the Christ, Prophet Mohammed, or Buddha?

This is where Hinduism stands out, as it outlines the presence of God both in gross form as Avatars, and in subtle form as an unseen all-pervading supreme consciousness.

Hinduism is beyond the religions – it's an umbrella under which all forms of faith can prosper. It's like the form of a democracy where each voice is heard. Thus, Hinduism is a like a library of universal consciousness and a pathway to access your final self-realization and liberation. It's not about human protocols as per the religious guidelines - it is about self-evolution and self-realization.

Self-discovery is the mantra here – and not about becoming a master of the religion!

All other religions were born out of the same one supreme consciousness as an Avatar; under different names at different places. Avatars like Jesus, Prophet Mohammed, Lord Buddha, and many others happened whenever a situation occurred due to which the sustenance of the Samsara (human eco system) was in peril. Thus, the Sanskrit epithet (sloka) -

Yada Yada hi Dharmesya
Glani Bhavati Bharata.
Abhyutthanam Dharmasya
Tadatmanam Srijamyaham.
Paritranay Sadhunam
Vinashay chu Dushkritam.
Dharmasansthapanarthai
Sambhabani Yuge Yuge.

The above 'Sloka' was recited by Lord Krishna in the Bhagavat Gita, assuring Arjuna that, "Whenever the acts of 'Adharm' (evil) create chaos on Earth, I come as an Avatar to restore 'Dharma' (faith), and put an end to all the evil."

It's important to note that each religion was born at different specific places that demanded some urgent reforms for sustenance of law and order. Hence the religions too, were a reflection of the background of the social structure that prevailed where the religion was born.

Yet it may not have been so, when it all began. As per ancient Hindu scriptures such as the Vedas and the Upanishads, there was just one umbrella under which human faith was sheltered. It was not any individual religion - but was under the wisdom of 'Satyam' (truth) of the Universe towards lifestyle management.

Hinduism earlier was such a shelter of faith that provided all living beings the sanctuary of providence.

With each passing Yuga, humanity distanced itself from God and thus the need for a more pronounced enforcement of law were needed in the form of religions, depending on the prevailing state of chaos in different parts of the world.

And after passage of time and the Yugas, in our present Kali Yuga, religions have become proprietary power centers of enforcement for civil code of conduct.

Hinduism was never a religion. It was a way of life that took every living being under its shelter.

Gods and Goddesses were envisioned in many shapes, forms and sizes, and accordingly their 'Deities' were sculptured and placed in temples.

Thus, Hinduism gradually manifested as a religion, and amidst the usual bickering for supremacy, numerous sects sprung up and became a part of Hinduism.

And like most other religions, Hinduism too gave birth to a number of siblings, such as Buddhism, Jainism, Sikhism, and quite a number of sub-sects amidst them.

Yet Hinduism retained some of the imprints of each passing Yuga, and the faith and 'God connect' during the passage of time.

The biggest imprint of the original concept of Hinduism still prevailed through the Vedic scriptures that taught us the sciences of 'Ashtanga Yoga', 'Ayurveda', and many others.

Over a hundred thousand ancient temples that carry forward the culture and belief systems over thousands of years continue to do so even till now.

The invaluable gift of Yoga is one of the many limbs of ancient Hindu culture among many others, such as the 'Vedic Math', 'Vedic Astrology', 'Tantra Vigyan' - knowledge of patterns of universal energies underlying visible and unvisible worlds, 'Vastu' – science of space and placement of the stars, and last but not the least, the science of 'Yoga' and 'Vedanta Philosophy' that were a part of all that were passed on from outside of the ambit of the Hinduism the religion per se, but from out of the concept of Hinduism as the whole.

In the first of the four Yugas, i.e. the 'Satya Yuga', humans were closest to God, and their work depicted wisdom of the highest order.

The rishis of those days (like scientists in our times), were gifted beings with divine wisdom who explained every aspect and dimension of God's creation. Each rishi was like a God designate scientist, and their work were a complete science, unlike our present-day scientists who are still grappling with one form of discovery to another each passing day.

The vast canvas of Indian faith bloomed through thousands of ancient temples – some dating back to 5,000 years, and many others that stood for as long as 20,000 years!

The architectural skill and technology used while building those temples are still a mystery even now. Not only the designs of the architecture of those times are mesmerizing, but the technologies also used in those times are mind boggling too! It's still not known as to how stone blocks weighing hundreds of tons were carried up to the hill top, and placed in symmetrical and yet intricate designs and carvings were made depicting stories of the era.

There are roughly seven hundred thousand temples in India; and each one of them has an independent architectural style.

It's not only about the style and the design of these temples that carried on its shoulders the continuity of ancient Vedic wisdom through the ages. These temples have stood through thousands of years of time without even a crack or damage on them. That shows the kind of durability of materials used, and technology used for their construction.

No wonder, thousands of researchers and archeologists throng at these sites in India from all across the world – to see for themselves and wonder about our amazing ancestors.

Temples with Unique Features and Background History:-

The concept of Hinduism as 'Life Sciences' had engulfed a major chunk of Asia in ancient times – extending up to Indonesia, Cambodia, Vietnam and Malaysia in the East, and up to the Persian Gulf and Iran in the West.

The Mayan civilization in the South American continent too is believed to have had links to our Hindu culture.

Relics of Indian temples are still seen in places mentioned above, and stamps of Hindu philosophy are still alive in socio-cultural lifestyle.

Every corner in India with their own culture and lifestyle had their own temples dedicated to their Gods, Goddesses and Avatars who played a role as their principal deity, yet the original philosophy and Gods remained the same.

The main Triad of Gods – Lord Brahma, Vishnu, and Shiva remained as the Creator, Sustainer, and Destroyer of the Yugas. Hence the temples of the trio prevailed in each and every corner of the country.

Brahma, the third of the triad is not worshipped in temples in a wider sense of the term because of conflicting reasons and belief systems.

The most common temples are that of Lord Vishnu in various forms and Avatars, such as Sri Krishna, Lord Rama, Lord Jagannath, Hayagrib Madhaba, Venkatashwera, Ayappa, and many such.

Lord Shiva, and his family members lived at the Kailash Parvat along with Lord Ganesh, Goddess Parvati (in many forms), Lord Kartikeya, Nandi etc.

Accordingly, thousands of pilgrimage centers sprung up across the Yugas as a conduit that carried the legacy of Vedic wisdom and the truths of the Gods.

The Char Dhams (four main centers of pilgrimage) – Kedarnath (Lord Shiva), Badrinath (Lord Vishnu), Gangotri, and Yamunotri; Kashi Vishwanath (Lord Shiva), Jagannath Temple (Lord Krishna), Tirupati Balaji (Lord Vishnu), Ayappa (son of Lord Shiva and Vishnu), Murugan (Kartikeya – son of Lord Shiva), Lord Ganesha (son of Goddess Parvati), the twelve Jyotirlingas of Lord Shiva – Pashupati in Nepal, Kedarnath in Uttarakhand, Kashi Vishwanath, Maha Kaleswar in Ujjain in Madhya pradesh, Omkareswar in Madhya Pradesh, Somnath in Gujrat, Mallikarjuna in Andhra Pradesh, Nageswara in Gujrat,

Trimbakeswara in Nasik, Madhya Pradesh, Grismeswara in Aurangabad, Maharashtra, Bhimshankara, in Pune, Maharashtra, Rameswaram in Tamil Nadu, and Vaidyanath in Jharkhand etc are just a few that draws millions to quench the thirst of their faith and belief systems.

In the context of the above, also flourished yet another aspect of the scientific skill and wisdom of the generations of the yester era that leaves even our present generation spellbound in awe and disbelief – that of the skill and the advanced technology of those era.

The engineering and architectural skill of amazing craftsmanship in each one of these temples, makes one wonder as to how advanced they were!

Their meticulous selection of site and location for the temples on the basis of astute astrological and mathematical calculations still makes one wonder in disbelief.

To name a few such architectural marvels across the hills and plains of India that standout in terms of tourism and spiritual interest:

The Hanging Pillar of the Lepakshi Temple:

The wonder of the hanging pillar of the Lepakshi temple in Andhra Padesh India is a mystery that defies logic. One of the 70 pillars of the temple, cut out from solid rock and hanging from the ceiling is something to be believed. Visitors often test the hanging pillar by passing a sheet of cloth from one side of the pillar across to the other side on the floor below the pillar to verify the fact that there is indeed a gap between the bottom of the pillar and the floor.

The beautiful carvings on the walls of this temple depict the story of the bird Jatayu who fought the Demon King Ravana to stop him from kidnapping Sita, wife of Lord Rama, as described in the Treta Yug epic Ramayana, and where Lord Rama came to know from Jatayu that it was Ravana who kidnapped Mata Sita.

Kailasnathar Temple in Kanchipuram:

This eighth century temple was built by Pallava King Narasimhavarman II, in the state of Tamil Nadu, India. Built on the banks of the Vegavathi river in 700-728 CE, it is a shining example of Dravidian architecture. Two prominent features of this type of architecture that were later followed by most of the Pallava temple structures are – the pillars and pilasters with a symbolic lion or a horned lion base (Simhapada, or Vyalapada), and plinth of granite for stability to the structure, and to prevent seepage. The 'Garbha-Griha' (sanctum-sanctorum) houses the main deity, a 2.5 meter high and sixteen faced polished black stone 'Linga'. The surrounding walls and the skirting of the walls adorn intricate carvings on the stone depicting celestial figures and sculptured statues of Shiva's various avatars namely Dakshinamurthy, Bhikashatanmurthy, Tripurantakamurth, Kalasamharamurthy, Gangadharamurthy, and Urdhtandavamurthy to name just a few, flanked by other deities such as Brahma, and Vishnu. The placement of the main Shiva Lingam is as per superior mathematical calculations of astrological concepts that augmented the 'Purush' and 'Prakriti' (male-female energies) harmony in the Samsara.

Mahabodhi Temple:

This temple, or more commonly known as the 'Stupa' at Bodh Gaya is one of the 84,000 shrines erected by 'King Ashoka The Great' in the 3rd century BC. Mahabodhi Mahavihara is the sole surviving example of what was once an architectural genre, is a magnificent structure whose creation is still a mystery and inspires millions of visitors from across the globe for spiritual salvation even today.

Sri Arulmigu Ramanathswami Temple:

It is a magnificent architectural marvel, located at serene islands of Rameswaram in the southern part of India, and is said to be one of the biggest functioning Hindu temples in the world. Dedicated to Lord Shiva as one of the twelve Jyotir Lingas, the Linga was established by Lord Rama prior to his war with the demon King Ravana. It is also popularly known as the Rameswaram Temple, and millions of visitors throng this temple simply to marvel at the awe-inspiring majestic architecture.

The Jagannath Temple at Puri:

This is yet another example of magnificent architecture with monolithic pillar with sixteen facets that stand in front of the main entrance. Two large lions stand guard at the entrance.

The temple is believed to be built by 'Vishwakarma' - the God of Engineering and Architecture. The anecdote goes that Lord Vishwakarma agreed to build the temple for the King under the condition that under no conditions he should be disturbed during the course of construction of the temple. The deities of the temple are Lord Krishna, his brother Balram, and his sister Subhadra.

It so happened that the King was worried about the safety and wellness of Vishwakarma due to the prolonged duration of time Vishwakarma spent alone at the construction site and hence went to check if everything was all right.

Lord Vishwakarma became very angry at this intrusion and left without completing the final phases of the job. And that is the reason the statues of deities in the temple remained incomplete!

There are a number of paranormal aspects of this temple, which are still as mysterious as the history behind the temple itself. For example, the flag atop the dome of the temple always flies against the direction of the wind. Nothing can fly over the dome of the temple. How the colossal Chakra (supposedly the 'Sudarsan Chakra' that belonged to Lord Krishna)- a massive metal structure weighing in tons, stands atop the dome of the temple, is a wonder.

For the last 1800 years, it has been a custom in the temple to replace the flag by climbing to the 45-story high dome of the temple.

Last but not the least, the most amazing feature of this temple is that in no way, shape or form this temple casts any shadow!

Finally, the Mahaprasad, or 'Bhog' (56 types of food offering made to Lord Jagannath) is cooked in earthen pots that are placed one atop the other over the fire, thus making it look like a pillar. And it is also a record that the Prasad never goes wasted, and for the hungry one, the pot of food never gets empty till his hunger is satiated.

The Virupaksha Temple, and Vitthala at Hampi in Karnataka:

Dedicated to Lord Shiva, and Lord Vishnu, glorifies the golden period of the Vijayanagara Empire. It's also one of the 'World Heritage Sites' declared by UNESCO.

The Dravidian style of architecture boasted of musical pillars at the Vitthala (Lord Vishnu) temple, and a triangular geometric 'Sri-Yantra" concept at the Virupaksha Shiva temple.

Kamakhya Temple:

A center of Tantrism on the Nilachal Hill in the city of Guwahati in Assam, India, is also one of the 'Shakti-Peeths' out of 51 such across united India.

51 Shakti Peeths refers to the 51 body parts of Goddess Sati, Lord Shiva's spouse which fell at different locations when Lord Vishnu dismembered the dead body of Sati, while Lord Shiva was carrying it and refusing to release it.

There is also an anecdote associated with this temple – a powerful demon Narakasur wanted to marry Goddess Kamakhya and proposed to her. Goddess Kamakhya couldn't reject him because he was a great devotee. Hence in order to not disappoint him, Mata Kamakhya gave him a precondition, that if he could construct a passage from the bottom to top of the Nilachal hill and also construct temple for her at the top of the hill overnight, then she would accept his proposal.

The story goes that Narakasur did manage to complete the job before the Sunrise in the next morning, but some celestial powers cheated on Narakasur by making the cocks crow earlier that day indicating that dawn had broken, and hence Narakasur's plea to marry Mata Kamakhya was rejected.

This temple is also a highly energetic seat of Shiva-Tantrism, and sadhus from distant places visit the place to learn Tantrism.   It is said that anyone with a sincere prayer at the feet of Mata Kamakhya is always granted with her grace, and wishes get fulfilled.

The architecture with stone carved designs of celestial deities depicting stories of ancient era – and all achieved overnight is something to ponder about.

The pious stream of water at the Garbh-Griha is a proof of Mata's presence, as is so believed.

Kedarnath Temple:

It is situated at the bank of Mandakini river after it's confluence with Alaknanda river at Rudraprayag – one of the Five (Panch Prayag) shrines of Lord Shiva.

One of the main Chaar Dham shrines, Kedarnath temple has stood the test of time due to it's strong architectural technology. When the entire area of the Kedarnath region got wiped out during the recent cloud burst and deluge in June 2013, the temple itself stood unaffected. Nearly six thousand people around the settlements of Kedarnath died in that deluge.

Badrinath Temple:

This too is one of the 'Char Dhams' in India. Dedicated to Lord Vishnu. Badrinath Dham is located on the banks of the river Alaknanda at about 115 Kms from Kedarnath temple, dates back to (1750-500 BCE) as per Vedic scriptures.

Both Kedarnath and Badrinath temple are believed to be from the prehistoric era, some three thousand years BCE. They were built by the Pandavas during the Dwapar Yuga and was rebuilt by Adi Shankaracharya around 8th century AD. Adi Shankaracharya lived at this temple for six months to a year and the other six months at the Kedarnath temple.

Kandariya Mahadev Temple at Khazuraho:

This is another majestic symbol of Hindu temples. Built by Chandela kings around 1000 AD, its one of the largest, and sits on a ten-meter-high platform and it's 'Shikhara' (tomb) stands thirty meters tall. Intricate stone carvings of mystical figures of deities such as Ashtadikpal, Saptamatruka, Lord Ganesh, Narasimha, Shiva and Parvati adorn the walls of the temple.

A horizontal belt of carved figures above, are erotic sculptures of couples involved coitus activity which are explicitly depicted.

Khazuraho attracts tourists from across the globe for it's amazing temples and architectural display.

Konarak Temple:

It is situated on the outskirts of the famous temple city of Puri in Odisha in India, and is another such temple, famous for its 'Chariot' believed to be drawn by the Sun God, and the components of the Chariot accurately indicates the time and hour of the day.

This amazing architecture was built somewhere around 1250 AD. The Chariot has 12 pairs of wheels that represent 12 months of the year, the 24 wheels indicating 24 hours of the day, and seven horses that pull the chariot indicates the seven days of the week. The eight spokes of each wheel indicate a span of three hours, hence eight spokes cover the 24 hours of the day.

The Sun-dial is astonishingly accurate, and is a major attraction of the Konarak temple. Apart from this, the temple also has intricate erotic postures sculptured on its rock walls.

The annual Konarak cultural festival attracts thousands of people from across the world.

Kailasha Temple at the Ellora Caves in Maharashtra:

It is the largest monolithic structure in the world! The entire temple is carved out of a single rock. It is believed that the entire temple was built by several dynasties over a period of 500 years and is influenced by several styles of architecture, such as Cholas, Chalukyas, and Pallava style.

The majestic ambiance of the Ajanta and Ellora Caves reminds us of the glory and rich culture of ancient era.

Brihadiswara Temple of Tanjavur:

Dedicated to Lord Shiva, this temple was built by Chola King – I, in the year 1000 AD, in a fully matured form of Dravidian architecture.

The amazing feat of installing a 80T single stone atop the Kumbam Sikhara (the tomb) of the temple defies our imagination as to how it was achieved in those days. Not that it is an easy task even today. And to top it, is the fact that the nearest source of the granite mine to build the temple was about 60 Kms away, so how did they manage all that amount of transportation?!

Basic Nature and Concepts of Indian Temples:

The evolution of Indian architectural styles goes back to more than 4500 years. The Indus Valley Civilization itself was recorded as early as 2600 years BC.

There are records of temples established in earlier Yugas, such as the Padmanabha Swami Temple at Thiruvanantapuram in the state of Kerela, India, is believed to be 20,000 years old!

The old Tirupati Srungara Vallabha Swami Temple in Andhra Pradesh goes back to 9,000 years.

The Guru Vayur Temple dedicated to a four armed avatar of Lord Vishnu in the state of Kerela is more than 5,000 years old. The fable goes that Lord Krishna wanted the idol of his beloved Vishnu to be protected and taken away from Dwarka where it was not safe. So, he asked his charioteer Uddhava to take it to some distant place where it would be safe and at the same time can be worshipped by the people.

Uddhava took the help of 'Vayu' – God of Wind, and Guru of Gods to take the idol to distant Thrichur District in the State of Kerela where it was placed and the temple of 'Guru Vayur' was established. The place itself then came to be known as Guru Vayur. The miracles of this temple are well documented, and inspite of being plundered repeatedly by the Dutch, and Tipu Sultan, it was rebuilt again and again, and the pilgrimage to this temple flourished as a major site also known as the Vaikuntham of Earth (Lord Vishnu's abode on Earth).

It is apparent, that time and age had no bearing on the on these temples, and nor did any impacts due to climatic disasters. A recent example of such an incident was in the year 2013 at the famous pilgrimage site of Kedarnath. A cloud burst, and flash floods swept away each and every settlement in the area, causing some 6000 deaths and millions of dollars' worth loss to habitation. And amidst all that calamity stood the temple of Lord Kedarnath (Lord Shiva) untouched and unblemished!

The temple of Goddess Jwalamukhi at Kangra Valley is another example, where the eternal flame burns without any fuel since thousands of years. Despite numerous scientific investigations the source of the perpetual flame remains a mystery.

There was no scientific logic ascribed to such a phenomenon, except for that it was an abode of God, establishing beyond any doubt about the presence of God.

Such stories of heavenly presence are dime a dozen with each and every ancient Indian temple, and the belief system in the minds of the Indian social structure is deeply ingrained.

Experiencing God amidst our Samsara is inevitable, and for the Aastika, God is only a blink away!

***

CHAPTER -XII

THE SCHOOL OF ELDERS

Siddhashram, also known as 'Gyanganj' as mentioned in earlier chapters refers to an elevated plane of consciousness, an abode for the spiritual masters. Siddhashram is also a link between humanity and divinity, and only a very few determined devotees make it to Siddhashram.

The question is why more number of people are not able to achieve that level of consciousness of Siddhashram?

Is it not possible for us ordinary folks to achieve that level of spiritual consciousness amidst normal ambience of Samsarik life?

The stumbling block is that 90% of us are drowned in the illusions of Maya and penchant for wealth and glory, where freeing the self from the clutches of the ego, and detachment from bondage is an impossible task.

Had there been a concerted effort by our society in that direction - to set up civic infrastructure to educate elders of the society to achieve elevated realms of consciousness, it could have been a great step forward for humanity to evolve.

It is quite a mystery as to why our society did everything to set up educational system only up to a limited level of adulthood, but not for the most important phase of life – old age.

We do not have any system in place for educating the elders post their retirement phase of life.

The result is that most of the elders in our society find themselves endowed with only a limited level of wisdom and having no sense of direction how to spend the last couple of decades of their lives.

It is very important to set up 'School of Elders' where they are made to realize their inherent potential after making them see the limited life that they have lived so far, and teach them how best to manage their old age, free from worries, anxiety, and taking care of their health care and wellness, and at the same time, giving them a sensible direction to improve their quality of life.

As per Hindu philosophy, a lifetime has been segregated into four stages – Childhood, Adulthood, Family life, and Vanaprastha.

Vanaprastha is a stage which is exactly the phase of post retirement, when a person will have completed all his familial duties, and obligations.

Vanaprastha is also an ideal phase when most elders become more focused on God, and spiritualism. That is probably so because of age related issues catching up on them, and making them weaker and dependent on others, loneliness, and feeling of insecurity hounds elders and they seek out old friends and groups where they feel more secure and supported.

This is a stage when the need for a dedicated social infrastructure for providing an educational system for the elders comes in, where one could learn the subtle wisdom of Life and become self-dependent.

We see numerous old age facilities made available with medical facilities and support system, but they only serve as a sustenance facility for the elders.

As per the principles of the Hindu philosophies, the Vanaprastha is a stage when a person learns to detach themselves from their families and the world of Maya, and seek the truths of God and non-duality.

The School of Elders would be a shot in the arm that would give a new lease of life to an otherwise life of despair and loneliness for the elderly.

This precious phase of life instead of being wasted doing nothing productive, and falling victims to numerous ailments such as dementia, depression, Alzheimer's, Parkinson's, or, that of loneliness, and dependency, should be the one of joy and pride for having lived life to its fullest, and wisely.

Old age is the most prized phase of life when a person can look back and see with clarity all the things that happened – the good things he did, the mistakes he made, and finally, the stupidity of it all - because the life lived till that moment didn't get him anywhere near to the finishing line of fulfillment!The School of Elders can have a number of educational faculties, such as - Wellness and Health care, Yoga and Spirituality for the spirituality inclined, facilitating training courses for those who are handicapped providing alternative options, and to teach basically how to escape from the shackles of their own ego, and widen the horizon of their consciousness beyond what they have been all this while.

This will provide clues to realize one's equation of karmic debts and credits which has a telling impact on after-death issues and writing the script of fate and destiny for his next life.

The School of Elders would be a step that would enable elders to perceive the world of the subtle – to experience the powerful influence of divinity on humans, and finally, to learn about the purpose of Life and the journey ahead to reach the destination – liberation of the soul!

The School of Elders shall be a symbolic representation of Vanaprastha stage, and can be positioned as the intermediate zone before the plane of Siddhashram.

"THE SCHOOL OF ELLDERS IS TO BE THE DOORWAY TO SIDDHASHRAM, JUST AS SIDDHASHRAM IS THE DOORWAY TO THE DIVINITY".

***

EPILOGUE

While our Samsara (the human eco system) sustains within the parameters of our karma and a pre-destined lifetime scripted out of our karma, yet there are thousands of those who dared to cross the limits of their destiny and liberate the self, from their pre-destined script, by transcending to higher planes of universal wisdom and consciousness.

While human karma is limited to our physical and material world of existence, our soul has the ability to transcend to a higher level of limitless universal consciousness.

In Hinduism, God is considered as an omnipresent 'Bindu' (point) of limitless consciousness, and one without any shape or size, one that is subtle and metaphysical. Our Soul (our true self) also happens to be a similar speck of consciousness like God but embodies a physical body to experience karma on its journey for liberation.

The awakening of the consciousness of one's inner self (soul-consciousness) is a process of expansion of awareness to transcend from the present level to an expanded level.

The 'Sanatana Dharma' of Hinduism refers to our soul as something that is indestructible. Even fire can't burn it, or an ocean cannot drown it.

The Soul, also known as the 'Atman' is born out of the 'Param-atman' – the supreme consciousness; also referred to as God.

The whole concept of the Samsara (the human eco system) is about the journey of the soul in one lifetime to another lifetime, and the evolution of the soul from a lower level of consciousness to a higher level of consciousness of the Param-atman, to achieve liberation, or Moksha from the cycle of birth and death.

During the process of this evolution, the self (atman) embodies a physical body for each lifetime to go through their karma – the expression of the soul's journey of evolution.

Moksha – Liberation of the Spirit:

In a general sense, all those sadhus and monks who renounced Samsara and spent a major part of their time in the Himalayan abode of spiritualism, are supposed to have taken to 'Sannyas' – a stage when after detachment from the ties of one's familial obligations (Dharma), the person leaves the playground of Samsara and walks the path of ascetic life to become a wandering monk – a 'Sannyasi'.

It is a harsh truth of life that we all come empty-handed and leave the Samsara empty-handed. Sannyasa is the path that illuminates this wisdom.

Sannyasa is stage when one re-aligns the soul's journey back to the main path and i.e towards salvation.

It is quite noticeable in Hindu philosophy that all the Gods, Devtas, the Rishis and Munis are married with their families. And a number of the legendary gurus and sadhus from the Himalayan belt too are married with their families.

And yet they were all liberated spirits!

Hence it is quite apparent that liberation of one's spirit is not in conflict with one's righteous karmic path of Samsarik life.

On the contrary, a liberated soul when united with the spouse, i.e. when 'Purush' and 'Prakriti' compliments each other, the liberation happens at a superior level of harmony.

The concept of 'Ardha-Narishwar', as discussed in the chapter of 'Vedic Covenant of Marriage' explains how 'Purush' - the pure consciousness, and the source of consciousness; and 'Prakriti' – that which is created, with a mind and a physical expression, are incomplete without the other.

In Hinduism, 'Shiva' and 'Shakti' represent the concepts of 'Purush' and 'Prakriti'.

In simple words, Purush and Prakriti are the male (wisdom version), and female (energy version) of the creation.

Love, the eternal essence of the creation, cannot be kept limited to the bonding of just the family unit. Love is universal and has no limitation. Hence Hindu philosophy propagates the four stages in one's life that depict the principles of one's Karmic Dharma –

1. **Brahmacharya** – the childhood, and adult phase of learning – enjoying parental love.
2. **Grihastha** – the family- household stage of life, enjoying the love of familial bonding.
3. **Vanaprastha** – the hermit stage, when the person learns to love every dimension of the creation as a whole.

4. *Sannyasa* – the detached ascetic wandering stage when the person transcends from experiencing human love to experiencing divine love.

These four stages of life are reflected in the lives of Ved and Malti, as described in this book, and in the first part of my book 'My Way On my Plate'.

Coming back to the lives of those sadhus and monks who renounce the world to come to the Himalayas, it's clear that they are in the 'Sannyasa' phase of their life, irrespective of their age whether young or old, experiencing the intoxicating divine nectar of love manifesting from out of their 'Bhakti' (deep devotion).

Some Sannyasis achieve the Sannyasa phase even at an early stage of their lives with their own free will. These are those ones who mastered the course of their own destiny and steered their journey to liberation as they saw fit.

Different Paths to Self-Realization:

There have been established facts that thousands of seekers achieved self-realization in numerous different ways, and hence it is true that all such paths to self-realization converge on one single point, and that is God-realization.

Hence it will not be wrong to say that the perception of God can be achieved in many different ways, and yet all of them lead to the same goal.

AASTIKA

Out of the numerous paths of Hindu spiritualism, some of the prominent ones are – Bhakti Yoga (devotion), Karma Yoga (action), Gyan Yoga, Raja Yoga, Kriya Hatha Yoga, and Tantra Yoga, Meditation, and Sri Vidya. These are various states of meditative kriya (procedures) followed in Hindu culture.

Yet, that is not to say that other paths of spiritualism do not exist.

Thousands of enlightened souls from the other parts of the world where Hindu philosophy is not practiced also have found God thorough focused devotion.

The simple logic to that is that, they too transcended from the detachment stage of life to the 'Sannyasa' stage of life, when their deep devotional power took them to Moksha (liberation). These are men of immense wisdom, and focused devotion to the truth that enabled them to cross the line.

It is about the soul connect to God – between the Atman (soul), and the Parm-atman (God).

The journey of one's life is about just that – to achieve soul-connect with God.

In this book we discussed about the sadhus, sanyasis, monks, and about the seekers in search of spiritualism going to the Himalayas to find their salvation.

These sadhus after having renounced the Samsarik world of familial life, devote themselves completely for the pursuance of God, and while doing that, goes through rigorous conditioning of the body, mind, and the soul at the Himalayan playground of spiritualism.

The conditioning empowers them with elevated level of consciousness, and abilities.

The severe freezing cold, low level oxygen, going food-less for months together are non-issues for them. They learn the intricate art of breathless living and can go into Samadhi at will.

The shelving of the body (Maha Samadhi) by some of these elevated sadhus has been recorded by a number of accomplished saints in their biographies.

Needless to say, that these siddha sannyasis mastered the concept of life and death, and could continue living life in the same body, or change over to a new life in a new body at will.

The concept of 'Mrityunjai' - that of conquering death may sound too pompous to us lesser mortals, but it is not so for those who are familiar with Indian spirituality.

There are numerous references to such liberated divine souls who have actually acquired immortality.

These elevated self-realized sannyasis had complete control over their life force energies (Prana), and hence steered their soul's journey as they saw fit.

Howsoever much these facts sound fictional, there have been many western researchers who have had firsthand experience about these sciences.

If we accept the life after death concept in Hinduism, where the soul continues to take rebirth one after the other, till such time when its journey is complete, then it also becomes clear that each rebirth of the soul is a karmic progression towards its final goal of liberation and self-realization.

The karmic progression also determines as to where the soul will take its next birth and live the type of life as per the pre-written script which we call as the person's destiny.

The destiny is a process by which the soul maintains an accountability of the person's positive karma, or negative karma.

The suffering in one's life is meant to neutralize the negative karma of the past and present life. Similarly, the good karma bring us prosperity.

Thus, the saying – *"What we give out, comes back to us!"*

In the overall perspective of Karma, the linear progression of good karma in life after life, enable us to become a superior self with higher wisdom, and thus dispelling ignorance from our lives.

Dharma - the righteous soul behind our Karma, should ride the chariot of Bhakti (the power of our devotion to God) to achieve our goal. Without a goal or a purpose, our Karma is rudderless and meaningless.

As stated earlier, the self-realized sannyasis who have acquired full control over life and death, write their own script of their destiny. They also have the ability to look back into their past lives and also see what the future holds for them. They also have the ability to help others by solving their problems.

Many cynic westerners have visited India from time to time to see for real and discover the truths about such sadhus and sannyasis.

One such cynic atheist reporter Paul Brunton in his famous book 'A Search in Secret India – The Classic work on seeking a Guru', recorded his in-depth study and firsthand experiences when he met and talked to such sadhus during his extensive detour of the Himalayan region.

Another book by the same author – 'Perspectives: Timeless way of Wisdom' also explores a creative wisdom of Eastern and Western ideas.

After his experience of deathlessness by withdrawing his breath completely as taught to him by a Himalayan Yogi called Brama, he declared – 'If I had not experienced this myself, I would have never believed that this was possible!'

Paul Brunton also wrote about a few such yogis in his book, such as Paramhans Yogananda, Mahavatar Babaji, Telanga Swami, Deva Raha Baba, etc. in his book.

Saadhu Tapasviji Maharaj lived for 185 years (1770-1955) by means of Kaya Kalpa – a means of cellular rejuvenation, three times during his life span. He also mentioned in his biography how he and his companion met a 5000-year-old yogi when he was travelling in the Himalayas.

Such references about the mystique Himalayan Yogis are countless, and it is natural that curiosity and disbelief about their prowess can never be appeased.

Hundreds of authors have tried from time to time to re-examine the scientific concepts behind those mysticism and traditions, and most often about the Himalayan spirituality.

Here I am not able to resist my temptation to mention about one such metaphysical persona from the Himalayan brigade of so many such others – Haidakhan Wale Baba!

Haidakhan, a shortened version of the original name for Hiriya Khand, is a small village near the hilly town of Nainital, in the state of Uttarakhand in India.

The name Haidakhan Wale Baba translates to – the Baba from Haidakhan village.

The mystery about Haidakhan Baba has been written about and described in multiple books and You-tube videos, and are not out of someone's figments of imagination.

Villagers recount how a 17-18 year old divine youth manifested from a floating Jyoti (a point of glowing light) around a cave near Hiriyakhand, and he walked right into their midst.

There were no pretentions about the youth – his glowing aura, his imposing presence, his shining radiance, and calm soothing presence was enough to establish the fact beyond any speck of doubt that he was a divine entity.

The most astonishing fact about Haidakhan Baba was that he manifested and also disappeared many a number of times.

His work, his sermons, and the hundreds of miracles that he performed are well recorded, and have been witnessed by not only his Indian disciples, but also by many western disciples who surrendered at his feet after they experienced his divinity.

Numerous western chronicles and journals in Germany, UK, and USA have discussed about Haidakhan Baba in their journals.

Well, who could have been Haidakhan Baba an Avatar of?

My guess would be who else but the Mahavatar Babaji, who conquered death at the age of 16, thousands of years ago, and about whom we have mentioned in our earlier chapters.

Welcome to the amazing world of Himalayan mysticism and 'Life of Spirituality' – in the ultimate School of Life!

***

Milton Keynes UK
Ingram Content Group UK Ltd.
UKHW030942261124
451566UK00018B/232/J